Leighann Dobbs

This is a work of fiction.

None of it is real. All names, places, and events are products of the author's imagination. Any resemblance to real names, places, or events are purely coincidental, and should not be construed as being real.

Table Of Contents

3

Chapter One

Celeste Blackmoore's white tennis shoes kicked up decades of dust from the dried timbers of the old saloon floor. The desert air felt suffocating, like being wrapped in a wool blanket on a hot summer day. The smell of dry wood filled her nostrils and scratched at her throat. Dust motes hung in the slats of light that shone through the gaps in the barn board siding and around the boarded up windows.

"Come join us, dear." Celeste whirled around in the direction of the voice. She squinted at the misty swirls of two figures that leaned against the bar, or what was left of it, at the other end of the room.

"Grandma?" Celeste recognized one of the swirls. She was used to seeing her grandmother, or rather her grandmother's ghost, but usually grandma wore the outfits Celeste had seen her wear when she was alive. Now, she was dressed as a saloon girl straight from an old western ... which was fitting since they were in an Old West ghost town, inside the remains of a saloon abandoned almost one hundred years ago.

"Yes, dear. You were expecting someone else?" Grandma winked. "Come meet my new friend, Deke."

Celeste walked toward her grandmother and the other ghost, carefully avoiding the gaping holes in the rotted floor. Deke dipped the brim of his cowboy hat at her. His pinstriped vest and dark pants gave him the air of a gentleman. Celeste guessed that type of outfit would have been described as "dapper" back in the 1870s. His ghostly form wasn't solid and Celeste could see through him straight back to the shard of glass that still remained in the mirror behind the bar where her own short-cropped blond hair and ice-blue eyes blinked back at her in reflection.

"Deke here was Sheriff of Dead Water back in 1878." Grandma grabbed the whiskey bottle from in front of her and poured swirling amber liquid into twin shot glasses that sat on the bar.

Celeste noticed the brass star pinned to Deke's vest and felt a tingle of interest spark in her stomach. "So, you were here during the stage coach robberies?"

Recovering the treasure stolen from those stagecoaches was the reason she and her sisters were in the town of Dead Water. It would be invaluable to get a lead on where it might be stashed from someone who lived here during that time.

She thought she saw Deke stiffen, although it was pretty hard to tell with a ghost.

"Yes Ma'am," he said. "What about them?"

"I was wondering if you might have an idea where the gold is buried," Celeste said. "It *is* still buried, right?"

"As far as I know." Deke tossed back his drink. "And I got a good idea who done it, too."

"Really? Who?" Celeste asked.

"Shorty Hanson," Deke said, slamming his shot glass on the bar.

Grandma poured more whiskey and put her hand on his arm. "And where would this Shorty have stashed all the loot?"

Deke narrowed his eyes at Grandma. "Well, out by his homestead, I reckon. But you be careful around him. He's dangerous."

Deke pulled out a pocket watch that was tethered by a fancy gold chain to a button on his vest. The sunlight glinted off the surface of the watch as he flipped it open. He glanced at the face quickly, and then clicked it shut and slipped it into his vest pocket.

"I gotta get going. Stagecoach is coming through and I gotta meet it."

He tipped his hat at Grandma, nodded to Celeste, and then pushed off from the bar. Heading toward the opening where the saloon door used to be, he glided over the hole in the floor and passed straight through Celeste, his form disappearing into a swirl of vapor before he reached the door.

Celeste looked back at Grandma who lifted the shot glass and downed the liquid inside, then scrunched up her face.

"Ahhh! That's strong stuff," she said. "Sorry about Deke, dear. He's stuck in 1878. I'm not sure he even realizes he's a ghost. But I do hope he helped you with your first clue."

"Yes. Thanks. Now we have a place to start, at least." Celeste's heart warmed—this wasn't the first time her grandmother had helped her out and it felt good to know that she was still looking out for her, even if she was a ghost.

"That's good dear. Now I've got to go ... there's a bridge tournament today and I can't be late." Grandma waved at Celeste, then disappeared into a swirl of white mist.

Celeste found herself alone in the saloon. A few droplets of water quickly evaporating on the surface of the bar were the only evidence of her grandmother's ghost having been there. She shook off the dream-like feeling that she always got when she talked to ghosts.

Did that really happen?

Turning toward the doorway Deke's ghost had disappeared through a few minutes earlier, her heartbeat picked up speed as she headed outside.

As she burst out into the deserted street of the old ghost town, a ripple of excitement ran through her. She couldn't wait to meet up with her sisters and tell them she had their first clue.

***

"So this ghost told you that someone named Shorty Hanson buried the gold from the robberies?" Celeste's sister Jolene's ice-blue eyes peered at her from behind her laptop.

"Yes. Well he said he thought Shorty was the one holding up the stagecoaches and figured it would be buried out by his homestead ... wherever that is." Celeste shrugged.

"Just how reliable are these ghosts?" Luke Hunter stood by the fireplace in their hotel room suite, his eyebrows raised over clear green eyes.

Celeste looked around the room. It was the main gathering room adjoining a suite of bedrooms they had rented for this "mission" and was decorated in a motif she could only call outdated western. The *Brandt Hotel* was more like a bed and breakfast than a modern hotel. It was over one hundred years old but their suite had apparently been updated sometime in the 1970s, resulting in a nauseating combination of plaid upholstered furniture, an orange shag rug and a small kitchenette in the corner with almond laminate cabinets and a Formica kitchen table. The big stone fireplace was a nice touch. Otherwise, the room was nothing to write home about, although it was more than adequate for their purposes.

Her three sisters, Jolene, Morgan and Fiona were in the room along with Fiona's boyfriend Jake and Morgan's boyfriend Luke. Jolene was bent over the laptop, her long chocolate curls dangling just over the keyboard where her fingers danced across the keys. Fiona and Morgan sat next to each other on the couch, their ice-blue eyes—a Blackmoore family trait—stared at Celeste awaiting her answer.

It wasn't surprising that Luke was concerned about the reliability of the information. He *was* in charge, after all. His job working for a mysterious cartel took him around the world searching out long forgotten treasures. On his last mission, the treasure had been buried in caves right under the Blackmoore sisters' seaside mansion in Noquitt, Maine, where the four girls had lived together since their parents' death years earlier. That's where he'd learned about their special "gifts". Each of the sisters had unusual abilities and Celeste's was that she talked to ghosts. Although the sisters were used to their abilities by now, Luke was still a little skeptical about how reliable they were.

Their gifts had not gone unnoticed by his bosses, who were a lot less skeptical then Luke. In fact, they'd requested the girls accompany him on this mission. They figured their unique paranormal skills might come in handy and it was looking like that might be true.

Celeste shrugged and answered his question. "As reliable as any *living* person."

"Well I guess we have nothing else to go on, so we'll start with this Shorty guy," Luke said. "How do we find out where his homestead is?"

"I'm researching the original layout of Dead Water and anything I can find about it online right now to see if I can figure it out," Jolene said from behind her computer.

"And I'll go out and ask around town." Jake sipped a cup of coffee as he leaned against the arm of the couch next to Fiona. Jake, a former police detective from Boston, had recently opened up a private investigator practice with Jolene as his assistant—asking questions around town was his specialty.

"While you guys are doing that, I'd like to take another trip into Dead Water with Morgan and

Fiona. Maybe we'll get some kind of vibe or something that will tell us more." Celeste looked at her two sisters who nodded. Morgan had a keen intuition that might pick something up and Fiona could bring some crystals that might give them a direction to look in.

"Meow!" Belladonna, their cat, jumped up onto Celeste's lap. She rubbed her pet's silky white ears. "Not you, Belladonna. You have to stay in the room."

Belladonna answered by narrowing her ice-blue eyes at Celeste, then abruptly turned and swished her tail in Celeste's face before she jumped down from the chair.

Morgan laughed. "I don't think she liked that answer."

Celeste watched the back end of the retreating feline. "I'm not sure we should have brought her ... she's never happy being cooped up inside."

"Of course we'd bring her!" Jolene interjected. "We couldn't leave her at home by herself."

"Or board her in a kennel," Fiona said as the cat jumped onto the arm of the couch next to her and playfully batted one of Fiona's long red curls. "She'd probably just escape anyway."

Celeste narrowed her eyes at the snow-white cat. She did have a way of escaping their house. No matter how carefully the girls locked her inside, she seemed to show up in the most unlikely places. But she'd been a family pet for as long as any of them could remember and no one wanted to go on the trip without her. So, they'd packed her in a carrier and flown her to the other side of the country. Celeste just hoped she wouldn't "escape" from the hotel room and get lost. She couldn't bear the thought of not being able to find her so far from home.

"Sounds good," Luke said. "I'm going into town with Buzz and see if we can get some metal detecting equipment. If the cache of gold is buried out in the desert, locating it with a detector could save us a lot of digging."

"Makes sense. Where are Buzz and Gordy anyway?" Morgan asked Luke.

"They went to check out the old mine." Buzz and Gordy were the "muscle" on Luke's team. They both kept a low profile, but sure did come in handy when they were needed to fight off bad guys. Celeste felt safer with them around, even if they were staying in a motel on the other side of town along with the third rental car.

"Well, it sounds like we have a plan." Celeste stood. Fiona and Morgan followed her lead.

"Do you need anything in town, Jo?" Morgan glanced at their younger sister as she took an elastic band out of her pocket and used it to tie her long jet-black hair into a ponytail.

"I'm all set." Jolene didn't even bother to look at them. She was too engrossed in digging up information on Dead Water and the stagecoach robberies.

Celeste headed for the door. "Then let's get going ... our ghost town awaits us."

Chapter Two

Celeste slid her hand along the smooth polished wood of the wide oak banister as they made their way down the stairway to the hotel foyer. In contrast to their sloppily renovated suite, the main part of the hotel still had most of its original fixtures and was loaded with antique charm.

Celeste admired the vintage wall sconces and stained glass window in the foyer below as she navigated the creaky stairs behind Morgan.

"I think it's my turn to drive." Fiona held her hand out for the keys.

Morgan stopped short in the middle of the stairs almost causing Celeste to collide with her.

"No way." She narrowed her eyes at Fiona. "You drove on the way here from the airport."

Fiona snatched her hand back. "Fine, but I get to drive on the way back." She tossed her red curls and hurried down the stairs two at a time.

Morgan looked at Celeste who shrugged. The two sisters had started fighting over who would drive as soon as they saw the white Cadillac Escalade Luke had rented for them while they were here in Nevada. Celeste could have cared less. She was happy to be a passenger and have time to gaze out over the desert landscape as they drove the ten minutes it took to get to the ghost town.

"Oh, I was looking for you guys earlier!"

Celeste turned to see Dixie Sumner, the owner of the hotel smiling out at them from the formal dining room where they'd enjoyed a delicious home-style dinner the night before.

"Oh?" Celeste raised a brow at Dixie as she stepped off the last stair.

"Yes." Dixie came out into the foyer wiping her hands on a towel she had hanging over her shoulder. "I have some treats for your cat—turkey giblets."

"Yech." Fiona made a face.

Dixie's cobalt blue eyes crinkled at the edges as she laughed. "Yeah, they are pretty gross, but cats love them. I cooked up some turkeys this morning and saved them for her in the fridge. Just pop into the kitchen and ask the chef, Dave, for them whenever you want."

"Okay. Thanks," Morgan said.

"That was really nice of you," Celeste added.

"Oh, well, I'm an animal lover and I heard her meowing up there while you were all out this morning so I figured some treats might keep her happy."

16

"Oh I hope that's not a problem. She didn't bother any of the guests, did she?" Celeste felt a tug at her heart. She hoped no one had complained about the cat.

"Oh pfft." Dixie waved her hand in the air. "She's not a problem. Besides, in case you guys haven't noticed, there aren't many people here to complain."

"I had noticed that," Morgan said. "Is it the off season?"

Dixie's smile faltered. "Well, that and Sheriff Kane seems hell-bent on doing whatever he can to make sure I go out of business."

"Is that the sheriff here? Why would he want you to go out of business?" Fiona asked.

"I have no idea." Dixie brushed a strand of gray streaked ash-blond hair out of her face. Celeste noticed her hands were red and rough—working hands. She felt a sudden twinge of compassion for the woman. From what Celeste could tell the pretty, middle-aged hotel owner worked hard for what she had. Why would the Sheriff want to close her down?

"But anyway, that's not anything for you guys to worry about." Dixie's face brightened. "Where are you headed off to today?"

"We're heading into the ghost town—Dead Water." Celeste saw a cloud pass over Dixie's face as soon as the words were out of her mouth. "What's the matter?"

"Oh, nothing. That place creeps me out." Dixie laughed nervously. "I've heard some strange things down there … especially near the old mines." Dixie slapped the towel back over her shoulder and started off toward the dining room. "You gals be careful out there, rumor is that place is haunted."

"That's exactly why we're going there," Celeste said softly as she turned and headed for the car.

***

Celeste stared at the old sign that marked the cutoff for the ghost town. Dead Water—1876. It had been a thriving mining town in the late 1800s but once the gold and silver ran out in the early 1900s the inhabitants started to move on. By the 1930s, the town was abandoned except for a few old miners who hung on, eking out a living from the few nuggets they could persuade the mine to give up.

No one had lived in Dead Water for eighty years or more. The homes around the town had all been reduced to piles of rotted wood decades ago, but some of the buildings on the main street were still partially standing. Like the saloon Celeste had been in that morning.

Morgan parked at the end of what was left of Main Street. Buildings in various states of disrepair dotted both sides of the street. The saloon, a country store, the front facade of what must have been a hotel. At one end was what was left of the Sheriff's office and jail, which stood next to the remains of the bank and the two remaining walls of the brick vault.

The girls got out and stood in the middle of the town. In the distance, Celeste could see the hills that housed the mines. The landscape was flat with humps of sand here and there, which she assumed were the remnants of old buildings. Other than the three girls, the place was deserted ... unless there were ghosts.

Celeste turned to Morgan. "Are you getting any vibes or anything?"

Morgan scrunched up her face in concentration. She usually got a "feeling" about certain situations and over the past summer, the sisters had learned to trust those feelings. She shook her head. "Nothing."

"Where did you see that ghost of the sheriff?" Fiona asked. "Maybe if we go there we'll see him and can ask more questions."

"In the saloon." Celeste pointed to one of the few buildings that still had all four walls and a roof. The front of the building had a rectangular portion in the middle that was taller and Celeste could still see remnants of the old saloon sign. Boards lay scattered in front where there was once a wooden porch. A few turned wooden posts that originally held a balcony over the porch still stood, but the balcony was long gone.

Celeste could picture swinging saloon doors in the wide opening at the front as they walked toward it. Stepping inside, the room looked exactly as she had left it.

The floorboards creaked and sagged alarmingly as the girls walked further into the large room. Celeste squinted, waiting for her eyes to get used to the dim light.

"Grandma and Deke were over at the bar." She pointed toward the end of the room where half of a bar remained.

"Grandma was at the bar?" Fiona asked.

"Yep. She had on a saloon girl dress, too." Celeste felt her lips curl in a smile. Grandma's ghost was full of entertaining surprises. "And she slugged down some whiskey from a shot glass ... or at least I think it was whiskey."

Morgan snorted. "Grandma? I can't picture her doing that."

"I think she was bringing the ghost to me," Celeste said. "She said he was stuck in 1878 and she wasn't even sure he knew he *was* a ghost. Maybe she had to dress the part to get him to talk."

"Or maybe she just thought it would be fun," Fiona added.

Celeste laughed. "Probably. But she's not here now and neither is Deke."

Morgan turned around, looking at the room. "This place is pretty cool though. I'm surprised it's held up so well."

"I wish the second floor was still intact." Fiona looked up at the large holes in the ceiling where one could see up to the trussed roof. Celeste followed her gaze, angling her head to the right so she could see the old wallpaper hanging from one of the few walls left standing.

"I wonder what was up there ... was this a brothel too?" Morgan asked.

Celeste shrugged. "Weren't they all?"

Fiona crossed to the opposite corner where the top of a stairway hung from the second floor. The bottom half of the stairs had fallen down and lay in pieces on the floor, but the top six steps had remained attached to the wall and hung there as if suspended in air.

Fiona picked up an ornately carved mahogany post. "These stairs must have been really nice back in the day."

Celeste was about to answer when a swirly mist on the top stair caught her attention.

Was that a ghost?

She grabbed Morgan's arm. "I think I see a ghost." Celeste stared at the stairs as the misty figure descended. The ghost wasn't taking shape very well and Celeste could only see a slight image, but it appeared to be a woman with a long swirly dress.

Fiona and Morgan couldn't see the ghost, but they followed Celeste's eyes to the stairs.

"Hello?" Celeste ventured.

The ghost hesitated, turned in Celeste's direction for a second, and then continued toward the saloon door.

"That was a different ghost ... a woman," Celeste whispered. "I don't think she heard me—she went out to the street."

"Well, let's follow her," Fiona said and led the way out the door. Once outside, Celeste looked up and down the street, squinting against the harsh glare of the sun.

"She's at the end, walking toward the hills." Celeste took off after the ghost with Morgan and Fiona following.

"Hello ... excuse me." Celeste tried to contact the ghost again but she was ignored. The ghost glided up a small hill and disappeared into an area sectioned off by a low, black iron fence ... a graveyard.

The graveyard was small with only twenty or thirty graves. Some had plain markers and some had fancy headstones. Celeste shivered as she glanced at one of the stones—a child's grave with an angel carved in the flat piece of slate that bore the child's name and age. She watched as the ghost floated slowly past the graves toward the back of the cemetery.

The area in back was flat with no tombstones. The sand was dotted with patches of grass and scrub. The ghost stopped at the very back and knelt down. Celeste could see the corner of some sort of plaque buried in the sand.

Was it a grave?

Celeste's heart tugged as she approached. The ghost was weeping soundlessly.

"Can I help you?" Celeste asked.

The ghost turned her face slowly toward Celeste. She was starting to take form now and Celeste could see she was a young woman in her twenties. Pretty. Long curls piled up on top of her head. She opened her mouth and one word came out.

"Vindication."

Icy fingers ran up Celeste's spine just before a white blur streaked between her legs and landed right on top of the grave.

"Belladonna!" Morgan gasped.

The cat landed in front of the ghost who shrank back and began to fade away.

"Wait ... vindication for what?" Celeste pleaded ... but the ghost had vanished.

Belladonna blinked at the sisters then turned and starting digging in the sand.

"Belladonna, stop that!" Morgan said and turned to Celeste and Fiona. "How did she get out here?"

Celeste stared at the cat. *How* did *she get out here and how did she even know where they were?* "Beats me. She seems to have a way of finding us."

Morgan shivered and rubbed her hands on her bare arms. "That's too strange. I hope we can get her in the car easily because I don't think I want to hang around here."

"Are you getting a vibe?" Celeste asked.

"Yeah. I feel ... unsettled. Like something bad happened here ... or is going to happen." Morgan shrugged. "I can't tell which."

"Well, whatever it is, it might have something to do with love." Fiona held out her wrist and Celeste raised her eyebrows at the pink stone glowing brightly on her sister's bracelet.

"That's rose quartz," Fiona said. "The gemstone of love."

Celeste frowned at the spot where the ghost had been. "Well, maybe our ghost was in love."

"Maybe." Morgan bent down to scoop up Belladonna.

"But what does that have to do with finding this cache of gold?" Fiona asked as they started back toward the car.

Celeste pressed her lips together. "I guess that's what we need to find out."

Chapter Three

Jolene Blackmoore closed the laptop, a satisfied smile lighting her face as she congratulated herself on digging up a good lead on Shorty Hanson ... too bad no one was around to share it with.

She frowned into the silence of the empty suite. Her sisters were back in Dead Water, Luke was in town and Jake was trying to find out whatever he could about the treasure, which meant all the cars were gone. The clock said it was past noon and luckily there was a nice little bar connected to the hotel. And, since bartenders usually knew everything, she could do a little extra detective work of her own.

She pulled worn, brown leather cowboy boots over her jeans and threw on an orange t-shirt then headed down the stairs and out the door. The entrance to the bar was on the other side of the hotel and she took a deep breath of fresh air as her boots scuffed across the dirt and gravel parking lot. The hotel room was air-conditioned but she found it a bit stuffy and kind of chilly. The desert sun felt good streaming down on her so she took her time walking to the bar.

Pulling the door to the bar open, she stood just inside the dimly lit room. The room was small, cozy almost. Tables and chairs sat against the walls, all of them empty except for one in the back where a thirty-something couple was engaged in intense conversation. In front of her, a long polished wooden bar beckoned. A white haired man sat on a stool at one end. Jolene slid into a seat three stools down from him.

The bartender looked to be in his late twenties. Tanned, tall and handsome, he flashed a lopsided smile at Jolene and she felt a prickle of interest.

"Hi, I'm Kyle, What can I get'cha?"

"What do you have on tap?" Jolene tilted her chin toward the metal handle of the beer tap dispenser feeling slightly disappointed he hadn't asked for id. Having just turned twenty-one, it was still fun for her to produce her license to prove it.

"We only have one beer here on tap ... Pabst Blue Ribbon."

Jolene made a face. "Are you kidding? People really drink that?"

The deep timbre of Kyle's laugh coaxed her scowl into a smile.

"I'm just kidding," he said. "You look like a Coors drinker, am I right?"

"Well actually I like Sam Adams but if you don't have that, Coors will do."

He pulled a glass beer mug from under the counter and turned to fill it. "Sam Adams?" he asked over his shoulder. "Are you from New England?"

Jolene nodded as he slid the mug across the bar to her. The foam topped golden liquid invited Jolene to take a sip, which she swirled around in her mouth for a few seconds enjoying the subtle bite of the malty flavor.

"You here on vacation?" Kyle polished a wine glass with a white bar towel.

Jolene shrugged. "You might say that." She looked up and saw him watching her with interest. Interest in her? ... Or in what she was doing here?

"Not much around here for vacationers."

"We're checking out Dead Water." Jolene watched two beads of condensation run down the beer glass and onto the bar before taking another swig.

"Dead Water? What could you possibly want there?" Kyle put down the glass he'd been working on and picked up another.

Jolene chewed on her bottom lip while she studied his energy, an unusual talent she'd discovered she had over the past year. She didn't see any dark colors in his aura—it was bright yellow, which meant he probably didn't have any hidden motives for asking about why she was there ... and also that he wasn't the type of guy for long term commitments.

She tilted her head, her long chocolate curls brushing against her arm. "My sisters and I are history buffs. We're here looking into the town history. Do you know anything about it?"

"I know it's been abandoned for a long time. We used to hang there sometimes when I was a kid."

Jolene sipped her beer and admired his biceps as he worked the cloth around the glass. She noticed the head of a dragon peeking out from under the sleeve of his gray t-shirt and wondered what the rest of the tattoo looked like.

"Anyway, it was a mining town and I think there was some kind of scandal back there a long time ago. But no one's lived there in decades," he said.

"The stage coach robberies," Jolene prompted.

"Yeah, something like that." Kyle slid the glass into the rack on top of the bar then placed his hands on the bar top and leaned toward her. His light gray eyes held hers and she felt a tingle zing up her spine.

"Don't let Sheriff Kane catch you out there though."

"Why?" she asked. "It's private land and we have permission from the owners."

Kyle pushed back from the bar and slapped the towel over his shoulder. "He always seemed pretty nasty about finding us out there ... but then again, we were just kids."

Jolene sipped more beer and watched Kyle pour whiskey into a shot glass and pop the top off a bottle of Bud he'd grabbed from the cooler. She thought about what Kyle had said. Was he trying to warn her off? Would they have trouble with this Sheriff Kane? It made sense the Sheriff wouldn't want kids trespassing—they tended to vandalize stuff. But Jolene and her sisters weren't kids and Luke had permission, so they shouldn't have a problem with this Sheriff.

"Anyway, Walter here knows a lot about Dead Water if you need a history lesson." Kyle tilted his head toward the man three seats down from Jolene, then walked down and placed the shot and beer in front of him.

"Hey Walt, this young lady here is looking into the history of Dead Water."

Walt slid his eyes over to Jolene who favored him with her best smile.

"Hi." She leaned over the two bar stools and stuck her hand out toward the old man.

"Hi there." His handshake was firm, his blue eyes kind. Judging by the lines on his face, he must have been nearing ninety, but Jolene couldn't be sure—the dessert air could be harsh on skin.

"What do you want to know?" Walt asked as Jolene slid into the seat next to him.

"I was just wondering about the history ... the mining and the stage coach robberies."

Walt lifted his left brow a fraction of an inch. "Well, that stuff's all in the history books, but what you can't find in there is the scandal."

"The scandal?" Jolene's brows shot up.

"Yep. My grandma told me the story when I was a little boy. She was just a girl back then, and maybe she romanticized it a bit, but she remembers a big scandal with the town sheriff and some woman ... something about a love triangle." His blue eyes twinkled at her.

Jolene smiled at him over the rim of her beer mug. "Sounds juicy. Did that have something to do with the robberies?"

Walt squeezed his eyes shut. "The robberies ... yes, I do remember my grandma talking about those too. It was right around the same time. The stagecoach used to pass near town ... carried all the gold and silver the miners had put in the bank, you know."

Jolene nodded.

"Anyway, I remember her saying how they caught the guy. Of course, he claimed he was innocent but the sheriff didn't believe him. Shot him right in the middle of the street. Scared her, she said." Walt shook his head. "Can you imagine the Sheriff shooting a man down in front of a young girl like that?"

Jolene shook her head. "That's awful. Did they ever find the gold he stole?"

"Nope. That was the big talk back then. Grandma said everyone went crazy trying to find it."

"I heard he lived right outside of town," Jolene said.

Walt scrunched up his face. "You know, I do think Grandma mentioned that. They dug all around there trying to find the treasure."

"Oh really?"

"Yep. The Sheriff tried to stop them from digging, but then *he* died not too long after that. My grandma said it was sad because he'd just been married ... or at least I *think* that's what she said." Walt chuckled and held his beer mug up. "Too much beer, and too many years does mess with a man's memory."

Jolene smiled while studying his aura. Turquoise. He was healthy as a horse and sharp in memory.

"Something tells me you don't have any problems with your memory," Jolene said. She gulped down the rest of her beer then pulled a wad of bills out of her pocket and slapped a twenty and some ones on the bar.

"This should take care of my beer and another round for my friend here." She pointed to Walt, and then glanced over at Kyle as she slid down from the stool and started toward the door.

"Thanks," he called after her. "Hey, I didn't catch your name."

"Jolene," she said over her shoulder as she reached for the door handle.

"Hope to see you around, Jolene," Kyle said and she shot him a smile as she tugged the door open and disappeared out into the hot sun.

He sure was cute, she thought, and then immediately dismissed the impulsive ideas that were creeping into her mind. There was a fat chance of anything happening with her over protective sisters and their boyfriends hanging around her day and night.

***

Jolene was halfway back to the hotel when the crunch of tires on gravel behind her caught her attention. Recognizing the big white SUV, she waved at her sisters, her eyes widening as they pulled to a stop and Morgan jumped out with Belladonna in her arms.

"You brought Belladonna with you?" She walked over to pet the cat who was wriggling to escape Morgan's captive embrace.

"No," Fiona answered. "She just kind of showed up."

"What? How is that possible?" Jolene asked. "Dead Water is twenty miles from here."

"You tell me," Morgan said.

"Meow!" Belladonna twisted and squirmed. Wriggling free of Morgan's arms, she dropped to the ground looked up at the girls, and started cleaning herself.

"I don't know about her." Jolene pursed her lips at the cat, then turned her attention from the cat to her sisters. "Did you guys find any clues?"

Morgan, Fiona and Celeste exchanged a glance.

"We found out *something* ... I'm just not sure it has anything to do with the treasure," Celeste said. "What about you?"

"I might have found where Shorty lived and got a little history lesson from a new friend." Jolene tilted her head toward the bar.

"You were in the bar all this time?" Morgan asked.

"Not *all* this time. I finished my research and went over for a beer." Jolene smiled. "Turns out it was a good move because I met someone whose grandmother lived in Dead Water back in the 1800s."

"Oh?" Morgan arched a finely plucked brow. "He must be quite old."

"Yes, but sharp as a tack." Jolene brushed a bead of sweat from her forehead. The desert sun was much stronger than back home in Maine. "Let's go inside and we can discuss what we found."

The sister's murmured assent and Belladonna led them toward the door, then up the stairs to their suite.

"Guess she knows where our temporary home is," Fiona said.

"Yeah, well I just hope she can find it if she gets lost." Celeste's face was pinched with concern. "We need to check the suite and see how she got out. I don't want her wandering all around Nevada alone."

Fiona unlocked the door and Belladonna streaked in making a beeline for her food dish where she sat blinking impatiently at the sisters.

"Don't worry Belladonna, we'll feed you." Celeste rolled her eyes at the cat, then pulled a bag of dry cat food out of the cabinet and poured some into the cat's bowl.

Belladonna sniffed at it daintily. After a few seconds, she turned up her nose and walked away. Jumping up on one of the chairs, she stared at the sisters sulkily.

Jolene couldn't help but laugh. "I guess she wants canned food."

"Or a mouse," Morgan said.

"Well, we have neither," Celeste answered. "She'll eat that if she gets hungry enough. Why don't you tell us what you found in your research?"

Jolene crossed over to the laptop, which flickered to life when she flipped up the top. "I was able to find out that Shorty Hanson lived about a mile outside of Dead Water. I imagine his homestead is long gone but I don't think anything new has been built there."

She pulled up the satellite photo of the area and turned the screen to face her sisters.

Fiona leaned forward to inspect the photo. "Do you have any idea where in that area his house would have been?"

"Well I do have coordinates, but I'm not sure how accurate they are." Jolene tapped her finger on the piece of paper where she'd jotted down a longitude and latitude. "This is from research done twenty years ago and I'm not sure how the researchers determined where the house once was."

"We don't really know that he would have buried it near the house anyway," Celeste said.

"Buried what?" Luke said from the doorway.

"The treasure." Morgan pulled him inside and slipped her arms around his waist. "Did you get the detectors?"

"Yep, Buzz and Gordy are trying them out," Luke said. "So you found out where the treasure is?"

"Jolene did." Fiona pointed to the laptop screen.

"Excellent. Good work." Luke held his fist out toward Jolene for a fist bump, which she happily completed.

"And what about the story you heard?" Morgan asked.

"Story?" Luke wrinkled his brow at Jolene.

"I finished my research and you were all gone so I went next door for a beer," she said ignoring the looks of disapproval from her sisters and Luke. "I figured it would be a great place to get some stories on Dead Water from the locals."

"Was anyone there at this hour?" Fiona glanced at the clock, which showed it was late afternoon.

"Yep. The bartender was nice enough to introduce me to an old-timer whose lived here all his life." Jolene fought the flush that threatened to creep into her cheeks at the thought of Kyle. "He told me his grandmother lived in Dead Water back during the time of the robberies."

The door clicked open interrupting her and Jake slipped in.

"Hi." Jake greeted them. "Did I interrupt something?"

"Jolene was telling us a story about the treasure she heard from an old-timer in the bar," Fiona said as he deposited a kiss on her forehead.

Jake nodded. "Go on, then."

Jolene shrugged. "Well, I don't know if this will help us find the treasure or not, but he said that his grandmother remembered some kind of scandal and Shorty Hanson was the stagecoach robber. The sheriff shot him but the treasure was never recovered."

Jake nodded. "That's pretty much what I found out too. And lots of people think that Dead Water is haunted."

"It is." Celeste laughed. "I've seen a couple of ghosts there already."

"Too bad you didn't run into Shorty," Fiona said. "We could just ask him where the darn treasure is and be done with it."

Jolene agreed. They'd only been there a day and she already missed the briny smell of the ocean and their quaint seaside town. "You saw another ghost when you went back there?"

"A woman this time. But she didn't say much … she led us to the graveyard, then wept over a grave," Celeste said. "At least I think it was a grave. It was in the back with no tombstone."

"I'm not sure that can help us, but any information we have can't hurt." Luke disentangled himself from Morgan and walked over to the computer, staring down at the screen. "So this is about a mile out of Dead Water?"

"Yeah, here's the coordinates." Jolene handed him the paper.

"Awesome." He looked at the clock. "We have a couple of hours of daylight left. What do you guys think about heading over there with the metal detectors?"

"Sounds good to me," Jake said. "I've been wanting to learn how to run one of those things."

"Wait a minute," Morgan cut in. "Do we even know who owns this land? Don't we need permission before we go digging it up?"

Luke looked at Jolene and she grimaced. "That's the thing. I couldn't get any information on who owns it."

Luke glanced down at the laptop screen again. "There are no buildings or houses around except for this mobile home way over here." He pointed to a small rectangle at the edge of the screen. "So it's not like we'd be digging in anyone's yard."

"Right." Jolene agreed. "Besides we don't even know if anyone *does* own the land."

"Exactly," Luke said. "I say we go out and start detecting and then see what happens. Are you guys in?"

"I am," Jolene said, feeling her heartbeat speed up with the promise of excitement. "What's the worst thing that can happen?"

Chapter Four

Jolene's boots dug into the sand as she swung the heavy metal detector back and forth. Her arm ached and she switched to her other hand, regretting her insistence that she be able to use one of the detectors along with Luke and Jake. The darn thing was heavy and the work was boring.

Ten feet in front of her, Luke and Jake had their heads bent toward the ground, their detectors swinging in rhythmic arcs over the area Luke had marked in the sand. Her sisters were standing at the ready with small devices called probes, which would probe in the sand and pinpoint the location of any small metal items found by the detectors.

Jolene glanced enviously at Celeste, Morgan, and Fiona who chatted happily while waiting for someone to find something, and then bent her head to continue her monotonous quest. She was wondering if she'd be able to use her arm at all tomorrow when her headphones erupted in a series of chirps that indicated the detector had found something metal in the ground.

Fiona, Celeste and Morgan must have heard the chirps because they hurried over, holding their probes at the ready while they waited for Jolene to pinpoint the area. Jolene moved the detector over the spot in a cross pattern, until she had the source of the beeping triangulated, then made a mark in the sand so they would know where to start digging.

Fiona pulled a small spade out of her back pocket and dug out some sand tossing it aside. Morgan tilted her probe—a long round tube about one inch thick with a metal sensing component on the end that would hum and vibrate when it came close to metal—and poked it around in the pile Fiona had dug.

"It's not in the pile," she said.

Jolene ran the detector over the spot again to make sure she hadn't gotten a false reading. It beeped when she passed it over the right edge of the hole.

"It says something is under here ... but I'm not sure if it's anything large." Jolene squinted at the display on the detector trying to remember the instructions Luke had given barely an hour before. They were looking for the cache Shorty had buried, so it would be something big, she just couldn't remember what type of reading Luke said she should look for.

Fiona pushed the spade into the side of the hole and flipped out more sand. The girls had discovered that digging in the sand was nearly impossible as the hole instantly filled with sand from the side. Morgan probed the pile and shook her head. Fiona stuck her probe into the hole, moving it around.

"I've got something!" Fiona said.

Jolene, Celeste and Morgan squatted around the hole while Fiona dug, probed and dug some more. She reached her hand into the sand, her face puckering, then lighting up as she pulled out a round object.

Jolene's breath caught in her throat as Fiona's hand emerged from the sand with the ring. It was small—dainty—with a filigree setting and a pink stone that glowed brightly in Fiona's hand.

Jolene was so engrossed in the find that she didn't hear the footsteps slowly sneaking up behind them until the unmistakable sound of a shotgun being racked froze her blood.

"Stop right there. Stand up and turn around slowly." The voice was as harsh and scratchy as the desert sand beneath her.

Jolene saw surprise in her sisters' faces as they looked up. Just before she whirled around, she saw Fiona slip the ring into the pocket of her jeans.

Jolene's heart leapt into her throat as she came face to face with the double barrels of a shotgun. Peering around them, she could see an old woman with keen, clear sapphire eyes set in a face of wrinkled parchment framed by long ash-blonde hair streaked with gray holding the other end.

"You. Over here." The woman addressed Luke and Jake, jerking the gun barrel to indicate they stand to the left of the girls.

"Who are you people and what are you doing here?" Her narrowed eyes studied each of them in turn.

"We're just doing some metal detecting," Luke said, innocently.

The woman snorted. "Well, you're trespassing."

Luke spread his hands at his side. "I'm very sorry. We were under the impression no one owned this land."

"Well you were wrong. This is *my* land."

"And who are you?" Luke asked.

The woman stood rigid, the gun unwavering. "Ain't no business of yours."

Like turned on the charm trying to dazzle the old woman with his smile. "Well we sure didn't mean any harm."

"I got plenty of trouble with gold seekers out here. I reckon that's who you folks are." She glared at their metal detectors. "Trying to steal a bit of history ... and gold."

Jolene heard the faint sound of sirens and the old lady shuffled her feet. The gun wavered as she looked back over her shoulder down the long, flat stretch of road where flashing red and blue lights could be seen in the distance. "Now look what you done. Here comes that damn Sheriff."

Jolene relaxed as the old woman lowered the gun and they all stood there watching the police car approach. It skidded to a halt next to them, unnecessarily kicking up a plume of sand.

Jolene squinted against the bright blue lights on top of the car as she watched the Sheriff get out. He was tall and lean with a hard face. He studied them with hawk-like beady black eyes as he approached.

"What's going on here?" he asked.

"Nothing we need you for." The old lady practically spat the words at him. "These people were trespassing and I warned them off as is my right."

The sheriff glanced down at her shotgun, then up at her. "Now Emma, you know you're not supposed to shoot a shotgun so close to the road."

Emma rolled her eyes. "I wasn't going to shoot them."

The Sheriff narrowed his eyes at the metal detectors. "And what, exactly, are *you* people doing here?"

Luke shrugged. "Just some metal detecting. We're in a metal detecting club back East and we like to try new places. This looked like a good place."

The Sheriff lifted one brow slightly. "You won't find anything out here but sand and cactus," he said, then turned to Emma, "and you if you would just sell this place and move into town, you wouldn't have all this land to take care of or have to worry about trespassers."

Emma glared at the Sheriff. "This land has been in the family since 1870. I won't give it up, no matter how hard you try, Sheriff."

Jolene studied the Sheriff. A casual observer might have thought the Sheriff was trying to look out for the older woman's welfare. Trying to get her to move to someplace less demanding and safer. But Jolene could tell by the looks the two gave each other there was animosity between them. The Sheriff's brown aura gave away the fact that he had ulterior motives that had nothing to do with the woman's welfare.

"Anyway, I suggest you people move on … And Emma, I suggest you go back to your trailer." His dark eyes narrowed at the woman. "It might not be safe out here at night for an old woman."

Jolene felt a chill run up her spine at the way he said the words. She looked at Emma who stood ramrod straight, her eyes shooting invisible daggers at the Sheriff's back as he walked to his cruiser.

"Boy is that guy a jerk or what?" Jolene said.

Emma laughed. "You can say that again."

"I get the impression he's keen on you moving, but I can see you're healthy and hardy ... he's after something." Jolene felt it only right to warn the woman who seemed more than able to take care of herself.

Emma sighed. "I don't know why, but Sheriff Kane's been trying to get me to sell this land for a coon's age. He puts on an act that it's for my safety, but I'm no fool. I can tell he has other reasons."

"Sheriff Kane?" Morgan's forehead pleated as she turned to Celeste and Fiona. "Isn't that the Sheriff that Dixie said she thought was trying to put her out of business?"

Emma nodded. "You mean Dixie Sumner down at the hotel?"

"Yeah, we're staying there," Celeste answered. "She seems so nice and so do you. I wonder why the Sheriff seems to be against you."

"We're distant relations ... don't get along too well since there was trouble in the family." Emma pressed her lips together. "She seemed to be quite distraught when I saw her out at the mine."

"She was at the mine?" Celeste asked. "Why?"

"Same reason I was, I suppose." Emma shrugged. "Checking out the goings on out there."

"Well no doubt she was distraught," Fiona said. "I think she's got a lot riding on that hotel."

"She sure does," Emma replied.

"Well, we're sorry if we bothered you," Luke said. "We didn't mean to infringe on anyone's property. We'll be going now."

Jolene looked back at the cars and realized the woman had come on foot. *Where had she come from anyway?* Probably the trailer they'd seen in the satellite photo, but that was so far away and it was growing darker by the minute.

"Do you need a ride back?" she ventured. "It's getting dark out."

Emma's shoulders relaxed and her eyes softened. "That's nice of you to offer." She looked around the group. "Maybe I misjudged you folks. I just figured you were a bunch of greedy, inconsiderate treasure hunters."

Jolene glanced at Luke who looked down, kicking at the sand with his steel-toed boots. "No Ma'am. Were a different type of treasure hunter."

"Is that so?" Emma tensed. "I only know one kind."

"We're not in it to find treasure for ourselves. I work for an organization that recovers old treasure ... for historical purposes ... and I suppose they make a lot of money at it too." He held up his palm at the look on Emma's face. "But we don't take anything we don't have permission to take. Usually my company pays very well if they are interested in a treasure on private land."

Emma narrowed her eyes at him. "Well sure you would, but if it were on my land, I'd own all of it!"

"Not necessarily. Depends on where the treasure came from in the first place. For example, if it was stolen to begin with, then it might belong to the original owner," Jake said. "Anyway my company knows all the laws and goes through the proper legal channels to make sure everyone gets their due."

"Oh, well that does sound like you folks are on the up and up. Many have come here with those things," Emma pointed down at the metal detectors, "but none were nice like you folks. Anyway, I can tell you there's no treasure here."

"Really? We heard this was the location of the homestead of Shorty Hanson—one of the miners here back in the 1800s."

"Why would the treasure be buried near his homestead?" Emma asked.

"Well, he robbed several stagecoaches of their loads of silver and gold," Jake answered.

"Did he?" Emma tilted her head, her eyebrows lifting a fraction of an inch. "You folks might be wise not to believe everything you hear." She hefted the shotgun onto her shoulder, turned and walked away into the dark.

Chapter Five

Luke and Jake loaded the metal detectors in the back while Jolene, Fiona, Morgan and Celeste squished into the back seat of the Escalade. Jolene tried to claim a window seat but Fiona pushed her into the car first so she was forced in the middle next to Morgan, while Celeste and Fiona got the windows. Jolene said a silent prayer of thanks that she and her sisters were all thin as she wriggled in the seat trying to get comfortable ... it was a tight fit as it was.

"What do you think Emma meant by not believing what we hear?" Morgan asked as Luke pulled out onto the road.

"Seems like she thinks Shorty didn't bury the treasure there," Celeste answered.

Jolene scrunched her face up. "How would she know?"

Jake half turned in his seat to look back at Jolene. "It sounds like she's lived here her whole life. She said the land was in her family so she might have heard from her grandparents like that guy you met in the bar."

Jolene pressed her lips together. "I suppose that could be true. But if he didn't bury it there, we have a lot more work to do."

"Yeah, too bad all that digging was a bust," Luke said as he turned into the parking lot for the hotel.

"Not totally." Fiona pulled the ring out of her pocket. "We found this, but now I feel bad that we took it. I should have given it to Emma while we were there."

Luke pulled into a parking spot and he and Jake jumped out to unload the car. The dome light came on and Celeste reached across Morgan and Jolene to take the ring from Fiona.

"This is pretty. Looks like the same pink stone that was glowing in your bracelet at the graveyard," she said, handing it back.

"It is. Rose quartz." Fiona looked down at her wrist. "Neither of the stones are glowing now though."

"Do you mind?" Jolene jerked her head toward the door indicating that Celeste should get out. It was cramped on that bench seat.

"We should give that ring to the old lady," Morgan said as they walked up the steps to the hotel lobby.

"Yeah, we should," Luke said. "We'll take a trip out to her place and give it to her later. Right now we need to regroup and come up with Plan B."

The hotel was quiet as they walked through the lobby to the stairs that led to their suite. Jolene peeked into the dining room where several tables sat, but empty of diners.

"Dixie must not be serving any meals tonight," Morgan said echoing her thoughts as they traipsed up the stairs.

They piled up in line behind Luke who was about to put his key in the door when it cracked open on its own.

"Meow!"

Belladonna bolted through the door screeching and hissing.

"What the heck?" Luke said as everyone turned to look at the cat that had jumped onto the top of the wide banister.

He turned back to the door. "Someone's tampered with the lock."

Pushing it open, he stepped in and then stopped short, causing everyone to pile up behind him. Jolene's heart skipped when she looked in through the door—the entire place had been ransacked.

***

"Someone broke in!" Luke and Jake rushed into the room. Jake turned to the girls. "You guys stay out there, they could still be in here."

Jolene rolled her eyes at Fiona—they'd proven in the past that they were more than capable of taking care of themselves. Jolene had a special control over energy that went far beyond seeing people's auras and Fiona had used rocks and crystals as lethal weapons more than once.

Morgan put her hand on Jolene's arm, stopping her from rushing into the room. "Let them check it out ... I have a feeling it's empty." She leaned in and whispered in Jolene's ear. "If someone was here, I know you could kick their ass, but we'll let Luke and Jake think they've got this one."

Jolene sighed and nodded at Morgan who winked. Belladonna jumped down from the banister and weaved her way around Morgan's legs just as Luke and Jake came back to let them know the coast was clear.

Jolene's stomach sank as she looked around the suite. Drawers were ripped out, contents spilled on the floor. The cushions from the couch were slashed open and strewn everywhere. In the bedrooms, their clothes lay in piles, splattered with red paint.

"Check this out." Jolene turned at the sound of Celeste's wooden voice and her blood chilled. Someone had written "Get Out" in red paint on the wall.

"Okay, let's see if anything is missing," Jake said. "Everyone check their things."

Jolene went into her bedroom. The old suitcase she'd brought from home was still in the bottom of the closet. It had been her mother's and, even though it was a little outdated, it had a lot of pockets and compartments she found came in handy. She was glad the thieves hadn't taken it. She rifled through the pile and it looked like her clothes were still there, although most of them were ruined. With a start, she remembered her laptop and ran into the common room, her eyes scanning the desk for it. It wasn't there.

"My laptop is missing!" She ran over to the desk and looked all around on the floor, under the desk, in the drawers. No laptop.

She collapsed into the chair, her spirits draining.

Luke came out of the room he and Morgan shared, his face tight with anger. "They took all the files I had on the treasure."

"Nothing of mine is missing." Celeste threw one of the slashed cushions back on a chair and sat down.

"Our stuff is all here too—but most of our clothes are ruined," Fiona said.

Belladonna jumped up into Jolene's lap and she kissed the top of the cat's head. "I'm glad Belladonna wasn't hurt and we didn't have a lot of research done on the treasure."

"Yeah, but that laptop was expensive and it has your passwords on it," Jake said.

Jolene shook her head. "I had RoboForm encrypted so no one can log in to any of my accounts. But I'll get a new laptop tomorrow and change my passwords anyway."

"I don't understand who would do this," Morgan said. "What did they want?"

Luke looked around the room. "I don't know who would do this, but I'll tell you one thing ... whoever it is sure wants to stop us from looking for that treasure."

***

"Let's get this mess cleaned up." Celeste's heart tightened as she looked at the warning painted on the wall.

"Whoever did this is probably after the treasure too," Fiona said. "And if they are anything like the treasure hunters we've encountered in the past, they aren't going to stop at simply messing up our stuff and writing a warning."

"We need to be very careful from here on in." Morgan slid one of the kitchen drawers back into place and piled the silverware that was on the floor into the sink. "I have a feeling we're in danger … and there's more to this than just recovering a treasure."

Everyone looked at her warily—they'd learned to trust Morgan's "feelings" and Celeste knew her sister thought carefully before saying anything about them.

"I agree," Luke said. "So, in addition to finding the treasure, now we also have to figure out who did this."

"And we need to replace the laptop *and* try to get back all the information we've gathered so far," Jake added.

"I saved all my bookmarks to the cloud so I'll have most of the websites I researched marked." Jolene reached into her back pocket and pulled out a small black rectangular object. "*And* I saved all my notes to this flash drive so we won't have lost a thing … other than the laptop itself, of course."

"I'm going to pick up a full surveillance setup in town and have Buzz and Gordy help me get it installed in here this afternoon," Luke said. "If anyone else breaks in, we'll know who it is."

"I'd love to ask around town to see if anyone knows anything, but my reception the other day was only lukewarm. These folks are a tight lipped bunch." Jake sighed as he sorted through a pile of clothing. "It's not as easy getting information in a strange town as it is at home, I don't have any contacts here and I don't know a soul."

"I might have a contact or two," Jolene said.

"Really? We should talk to them," Jake replied.

"I think we should also talk to Dixie and see if she or her staff knows anything. Surely *someone* must have heard or seen something strange while we were out." Celeste frowned at the pile of paint stained clothes she had just sorted. "And I guess I need some new clothes."

"Me too," Fiona said. "I vote we finish cleaning up tonight and then go do some shopping tomorrow. We can talk to Dixie and whoever else was here before we head out."

Chapter Six

The next morning Luke, Jake, and Jolene headed off to find a store where they could buy electronics. Celeste, Morgan and Fiona sat, as best they could, on the slashed cushions in the living room.

"Dixie's going to need to paint in here." Celeste nodded toward the painted warning on the wall. They'd tried to scrub it off but it didn't make much of a difference.

"And buy new furniture." Fiona waved her hand around the room.

"I hope we can still stay here," Morgan said. "This is the only hotel close to Dead Water. All the others are on the other side of the city."

The Brandt Hotel had been built in 1880 when Dead Water was still thriving. It was about ten miles away from Dead Water and about another ten from the nearest town, Couver City. It stood on Route 51, which had once been a major thoroughfare. The addition of major highways to the area since had turned the traffic to a trickle and, as a result, the Brandt was now the only place between Dead Water and Couver City that was still in business.

Celeste loved the quaint details of the one hundred and forty year old hotel. She hated to think of it going out of business like many of the abandoned and dilapidated hotels, stores and gas stations that dotted that stretch of road.

Fiona plucked the keys to the Escalade from the kitchen table and dangled them in front of her. "Are you guys ready to go shopping? I do believe it's my turn to drive."

"Yep, let's head down and see if we can ferret Dixie out." Morgan led the way to the door.

Celeste peeked into her room to make sure Belladonna was still asleep on the bed, and then followed her sisters down the stairs.

Dixie wasn't hard to find. She was in the now empty dining room clearing dirty dishes from a table. The hotel owner looked like she hadn't slept all night, but managed a weak smile when she saw the sisters standing in the doorway.

"Just cleaning up after the other guest." She pointed to the crumbs on the table. Celeste's stomach growled—they hadn't had time to come down and eat the breakfast served by the hotel and she was hungry.

"Other guest?" Celeste felt the hair on her neck tingle. *Could that be who broke into their room?*

"Yes, a nice young man," Dixie said. "I'm grateful for any guests these days, the way things are going."

"Well, that's kind of what we wanted to talk to you about," Fiona said.

Dixie froze in place, staring at them. "What do you mean?"

The girls looked at each other not knowing how to break the news to her.

"Our suite was broken into last night," Morgan blurted out.

Dixie's eyes went wide. "What?" She looked from sister to sister, her blue eyes searching theirs.

"Yep," Celeste said. "They tore up the couch, tossed the place and then put paint on our clothes and wrote a message on the wall."

"We tried to clean it up the best we could ...," Fiona added.

Dixie sank into one of the wooden chairs, burying her face in her hands. "Who would do something like that?"

Celeste's heart tugged for the other woman. "We don't know."

Dixie closed her eyes and sighed. "I don't even know if I have any money to replace the couch. How bad is it?"

Celeste looked at Morgan and Fiona. Their eyes mirrored the sympathy she felt.

"Well, it's pretty bad, but we might have a lead on a free couch," Celeste lied.

Due to previously finding a valuable treasure buried under their three hundred year old house, the girls had more money than they could ever spend. They could well afford to buy Dixie a new couch and Celeste knew her sisters would agree. Besides, if it was someone trying to thwart *their* treasure detecting efforts, they owed it to her to replace what was damaged.

"What about your things. Were they ruined?" Dixie's eyes darted from one girl to the next. "I'll have to replace those for you. Can you even stay in the room?"

"It's okay." Morgan put her hand on Dixie's shoulder. "We didn't have anything valuable. The room can be fixed. In fact, we're going into town today and we'll get paint for the wall and everything. We just wanted to know if you saw who did it."

Dixie pressed her lips together. "I didn't see anything. Do you know what time it happened?"

"We got back just after dark, right?" Fiona turned to Morgan and Celeste.

Morgan nodded. "And we'd only been out a couple of hours ... so sometime between five and seven I'd say."

"I went into town around four," Dixie said. "There was a town meeting and I had some errands to run. It was about rezoning here which might shut down the hotel. I gave the staff the night off."

Celeste's forehead pleated. "How could they do that? Wouldn't you be grandfathered in?"

"In a normal town, yes. But here ..." Dixie shrugged.

"It sounds like you think someone has it in for the hotel," Morgan said.

"Well, it sure seems that way. My cousin, Marty, owned it and was letting it go to ruin. When he died, I bought it. The hotel was built by my great-grandfather and I couldn't bear to see it going to ruin. But ever since I bought it, there's been one setback after another with the town. It's almost like they want to just get rid of it."

Celeste's heart crunched as she looked around at the period details and architecture. "Why would anyone want that? This place should be restored as a piece of history."

Dixie shrugged. "My thoughts exactly. Anyway, I think Dave, the chef, was here last night. Let's go see if he's in the kitchen and we can ask."

She pushed up from the table and started toward a door in the back of the dining room. She pushed the door open and the girls followed her into a small kitchen. The smell of bacon spiced the air. The chrome fixtures, shelves and counters gleamed. White tile sparkled.

"Dave, these are some of our guests." A man in his late thirties looked up from a large pot he was stirring. He wore a white chef's jacket and his dark eyes sparkled as he greeted the girls.

"Their suite was broken into last night. You were here, right?" Dixie asked.

Dave's eyes registered alarm. "Yes. No one was hurt, I hope?"

"We weren't here," Morgan said. "But we were wondering if you heard anything."

Dave stopped stirring and pressed his lips together. "I was in here all night making the deserts for the next couple of days and had the mixer going ... it's loud."

"So you didn't hear or see anything?" Dixie asked.

"No. I'm sorry. I was so focused on baking," he said. "What time was that?"

"Between five and seven."

Dave pressed his lips together. "I did hear a car drive in, but when I looked out it was the new guest. The young man."

Celeste exchanged a look with her sisters. "Was he alone?"

"Yes."

Celeste frowned. She didn't think only one person had tossed the room, but this new guy still warranted checking out.

"Okay, thanks Dave." Dixie turned to the girls. "Sorry we couldn't be more help. I should come up and look at the suite ... and we should put a call in to the police."

Celeste remembered the unfriendly look in Sheriff Kane's eyes the night before. "What can they do? Probably nothing, right?"

Dixie rolled her eyes. "If it has to do with this place they'll probably be glad."

"Well then I think we can leave them out of it, right?" Celeste looked at her sisters who nodded. Celeste noticed that Dixie looked relieved.

They were almost out of the room when Dave called to them. "Are you the guests with the cat?"

Celeste turned and saw Dave at the fridge. The bag of slimy brown meat in his hand chased away the hunger she'd felt earlier. "Yes."

"Then I have these giblets for you."

Morgan went to retrieve the bag. Dixie played nervously with the cuff on her shirt. "I forgot all about your cat ... I hope she didn't get hurt in the break-in."

Celeste smiled at her. "Belladonna? Oh no, she's fine. In fact, I feel sorry for the intruders because if they tangled with her, I'm sure they didn't come out of it unscathed."

***

"Thanks for those turkey giblets," Morgan said as she closed the door to the suite after showing Dixie the damage.

"You're welcome. I hope Belladonna likes them, just don't feed her too much at one time. It could upset her digestion." Dixie bent down to inspect the lock, which had been jimmied open. "I'll get someone to fix this right away and someone at the front desk today to make sure no one goes in your rooms."

The sisters thanked her and they all went downstairs. Celeste headed toward the front door.

"Oh, before you leave, I have something I wanted to show you." Dixie had her hand on the knob of a beautiful oak door with a recessed stained glass panel that led to a room on the left of the staircase.

The girls turned toward her and she opened the door revealing a small library. Celeste followed her in. It was like going back in time. The room was lined with bookshelves filled with old books. The scent of decades old pipe smoke lingered in the folds of the thick mahogany-colored velvet curtains that flanked long sun streaked windows. The rich jewel tones of the oriental carpet provided a perfect balance to the brown leather chairs set in front of a carved marble fireplace.

"Wow." Morgan stood in the doorway, her eyes wide as she drank in the room.

"Isn't it beautiful?" Dixie smiled proudly. "It's one of the few rooms that didn't get renovated over the years. It's exactly as it was in 1880."

"I was hoping to restore the rest of the hotel to its original glory eventually." Dixie's face tightened as she looked around the room. "But that takes a lot of money and I've sunk most of what I have into it already."

Dixie crossed over to a bookshelf and pulled out a dark blue canvas bound book. "This here is a book about Dead Water back when the mines were working." She held the book out to Celeste. "It was written in 1889. I figured you might be interested in some of the information seeing as you were so interested in the town."

Celeste looked down at the heavy book—*The Story of Dead Water*. "This is great. I'm sure it will help us a lot."

"Okay, good." Dixie ushered them out to the foyer and closed the library door. "Feel free to read it while you're here. I just need it back as it's part of the library that my great-grandmother curated here when they built the hotel. I don't know if it's has monetary value, but it's got a lot of sentimental value to me."

"Of course." Celeste opened the book and thumbed through the crisp thick pages she couldn't wait to start reading. "I'll take good care of it."

She followed her sisters outside, her face still buried in the book, the slight smell of mildew tickled her nose. The sun was hot, as usual, and she could hear a car pulling out of the parking lot.

Beside her, she heard Morgan's sharp intake of breath.

"What?" Celeste looked up from the book to see her sister staring at the taillights of a Dodge that had just pulled onto the road.

"Did you see him?" Morgan asked.

"See who?" Fiona asked. "The guy in the car?"

"Yes ... did he look familiar to either of you?"

Celeste stared down the road but the car was too far away. "Sorry, I didn't see him. Who did you think it was?"

Morgan shook her head. "No one. It was just my imagination. This break-in thing has me a little spooked." Morgan slid into the passenger seat, leaving the back for Celeste.

"So anyway, where do you guys want to go shopping?" Morgan turned to her sisters and pretended like she'd forgotten about the guy in the car.

Celeste shrugged. "Where-ever."

Fiona started the SUV and pulled onto the road, heading in the opposite direction of the other car.

"So you don't want to tell us who you thought was in the car?" Celeste pressed.

"Car? What car?" Morgan joked. "Really it was just my overactive imagination. Let's focus on more interesting and fun things like shopping."

"If you say so," Celeste answered. But she wasn't fooled. Because if it really was nothing like Morgan insisted, then why did she keep glancing out the rear view mirror every ten seconds?

Chapter Seven

The girls got back from their shopping trip at the same time the delivery truck from Ace Furniture—the local furniture store the sisters had bought a replacement couch and chairs from—was pulling into the parking lot.

Fiona sprinted over to talk to the deliverymen—giving them instructions as to where to bring the furniture, Celeste presumed, as she watched Morgan glance around the parking lot uneasily.

"Looking for someone?" Celeste asked.

"No. Just looking around." Morgan flipped her long black hair over her shoulder as she grabbed the shopping bags from the back seat and headed toward the hotel door.

Celeste walked after her, the old book she'd been browsing through the whole trip clutched to her chest. She followed their new beige microfiber couch up the stairs and watched while the deliverymen exchanged the old set for the new. Fiona had made some sort of deal with them to take the ruined furniture away and Celeste breathed a sigh of relief when they finally disappeared with the last of it.

"This furniture looks great." Fiona plopped down into one of the chairs. "And it's a lot more comfortable too."

"Buzz fixed the lock and I've just about finished setting up this surveillance stuff." Luke said from atop a ladder where he was running a wire to a small camera. "Jolene's setting up the new computer we bought."

"So, did Dixie see or hear anything last night?" Jake's eyes went from Fiona, to Morgan to Celeste.

"No. Apparently, only the chef was here due to some big town meeting and he was busy in the kitchen. Didn't hear a thing." Morgan pressed her lips together. "But we did find out there is a mysterious guest that came in yesterday."

"Mysterious?" Jake's eyebrows lifted.

"Well, not really mysterious," Celeste said, "although Morgan seems to think so. It's just another guest. Some guy."

"And you think he is involved with this?" Jake asked Morgan.

"No. Not really," Morgan said. "I just have a funny feeling about him."

Celeste, Fiona and Jake exchanged a glance. Jolene looked up from the new laptop she was setting up on the table. "After everything I've seen, I wouldn't take *your* feelings lightly, Morgan."

"I'll look into this new guest," Jake said. "Now, someone help me move this couch out so I can paint the wall."

"Is he the only guest staying here besides us?" Jolene asked.

"Apparently," Fiona answered as she struggled to pick up the end of the couch opposite Jake. "I haven't seen anyone else."

"You know, I think it's sad that this place isn't doing well. It's a nice place, even though this suite could use some updating." Celeste settled into a chair and opened the book Dixie had given her. "I'd like to do something to get that Sheriff to back off. I feel sorry for Dixie."

Morgan came to Fiona's aid and the two of them moved their end of the couch away from the wall. "Did you find anything good in that book?"

"Book?" Jolene asked.

"Yeah, Dixie lent us a book on Dead Water." Celeste held the book up. "I was thinking it might have some clues to the treasure and it's actually very interesting. There are even some pictures."

Celeste opened the book to the last page she'd read—a section that talked about the various mines and different claims for each section of the mine. She read with interest; she knew little about mining and didn't realize that different people could purchase or stake claim to different areas of land to mine in.

That section of the book contained several glossy pages with pictures from the 1870s, which contained images of the people of Dead Water as well as the old mining tools and household items they used. She wondered what the tools and household items were, her heart clenching as she realized her boyfriend, Cal, would know exactly what each item was used for.

Cal Reed had been a friend of the family, and her best friend, since she was a kid. For most of their lives, that's all they'd been—friends. But the events of the past year had brought them together and somehow they'd turned into more than friends … much more.

Cal, who owned a thriving antique and pawn store, had business back home, otherwise he'd be here right beside her. Celeste missed him.

She sighed and turned back to the book. Until Cal could join them, she might as well bury herself in her work.

"So, what's next on the agenda?" Jake spread a canvas tarp over the floor and back of the couch, then took out some sandpaper and started on the wall.

"We still have some asking around to do, I think," Morgan said. "Did you ever talk to your contacts, Jolene?"

Jolene made a few exaggerated taps on her keyboard, then closed the laptop and stood. "I haven't had a chance, but now that I'm done setting this up, I think it's the perfect time to head on over and talk to them."

Luke hopped off the ladder and folded it up. "Our main objective is to find that treasure. I don't want to get sidetracked with looking for whoever broke in. We don't know *why* they did or if it even has anything to do with the treasure, but if it does, we'll probably find out soon enough without having to go looking for answers."

"Okay, so then where do we look?" Fiona asked. "Seems to me we're no closer to knowing where it is now than we were yesterday."

"Maybe we are." Celeste held up the book, the page open to a picture of a grizzled old miner with a long beard and long hair. "According to this book, this guy here is Shorty Hanson and he had rights to a mine ... mine number seven."

Fiona shrugged. "Yeah, so, there were a lot of miners back then."

"Sure, but I was thinking ... what better place to bury a cache of stolen treasure, than right in your own mine?"

Luke came over to look at the picture. "You know, that's not a bad idea. Gold and silver that the miners had cashed in to the bank was stolen from the stagecoaches. If he stashed the stolen nuggets in the mine and then brought them out little by little later on, no one would question it."

"It would be the perfect setup," Morgan said. "Just bury the cache and then come out with it a little bit at a time over the years."

"Absolutely. I think you're on to something, Celeste," Luke said. "Now if we can just figure out which mine is number seven, we might be in business."

***

Jolene changed into the new light blue tank top she'd bought to round out her wardrobe since most of it had been splattered with paint during the break-in. She glanced in the mirror, thankful she'd been wearing her favorite jeans and cowboy boots when the thieves had their paint party. She wasn't much of a clotheshorse but the jeans had taken a long time to break in perfectly, as had the boots, and she would have hated to lose them.

She rummaged in her bag for her makeup kit and before she knew what she was doing, she'd put a thick coating of black on her eyelashes, making her blue eyes stand out even more than usual. Feeling embarrassed with herself, she shoved the mascara back in her bag.

She didn't usually bother with makeup—why was she doing it now? Because she was heading to the bar? She hoped it wasn't because of the cute bartender, Kyle—surely, she couldn't have been *that* taken with him. She knew he wasn't boyfriend material and she wasn't the one-night-stand type. Tearing herself away from the mirror, she skidded out into the common room of the suite.

"I'm going to head over to the bar and see if my contacts know anything about the break-in while you guys are finishing up," she said as she hurried to the door.

"Umm ... okay. Do you want me to go with you?" Morgan asked.

Jolene rolled her eyes at her older sister who tended to be overprotective with good reason— their mother had jumped to her death from the cliffs outside their home when Jolene was only fourteen and Morgan, who had been twenty-eight at the time, had had to put herself in the role of mother. And since their father was already dead, her sisters had all chipped in to finish the parenting job. Jolene appreciated all they had done for her ... but she was twenty-one now and didn't need parenting anymore.

"I think I'll be fine ... I'll only be a few minutes while I'm waiting for you guys to get it together so we can go to the mine."

Morgan narrowed her eyes, but gave in. "Okay, see you in a bit, then."

Jolene slipped out of the door, ran down the stairs and out into the hot desert sun. It was late afternoon and the sun was shining directly into her face. She squinted and then put her hand up to shade her eyes, noticing a movement over by the bar.

Was that someone ducking behind the building?

"Hey! You!" She sprinted over to the building, skidding around the corner where she'd thought she'd seen the person go, but no one was there.

"What the heck?" Jolene scrunched up her face. She was sure she'd seen someone.

Walking back to the front of the building, she shrugged. *Probably just my imagination going wild due to the break-in*, she thought as she tugged open the door to the bar.

Inside, it was just as dim as the day before. She headed straight to the bar, letting her eyes adjust as she walked. As she slid onto a bar stool, she noticed the tables and other stools were empty. One lone glass sat at the end of the bar, empty except for a few ice cubes melting on the bottom.

"Hey there." Kyle had turned at the sound of the door opening and now leaned against the back bar smiling at her.

"Hey," she said.

"Coors?"

"That would be great."

He poured the beer and slid it across the bar to her along with a square white napkin. "Hey, some guy was just in here asking about you and your sisters."

Jolene's heart lurched. She whirled around to look at the door. "Did he just leave, like a few seconds ago?"

"Yes, right before you came in."

She turned back to look at Kyle and noticed he was leaning on the bar studying her intently. It made her a little nervous, but she couldn't pinpoint why. "What did he look like?"

Kyle shrugged. "Dark hair, kind of tall. Just a regular guy. I hope you're not in some kind of trouble."

"Nothing we can't handle," she said. "But our rooms did get broken into last night. Have you heard anything about that?"

A cloud passed over Kyle's face as he straightened back up. "No. Why would I know anything?"

"Well, I just figured you might have heard something here in the bar."

He shook his head. "No. You think that guy that was asking about you had something to do with it?"

"Maybe." Jolene sipped her beer, the grainy smell of hops tickled her nose while the icy beer cooled her throat.

"Did they take anything?" Kyle asked.

"Yeah. Computers and stuff."

"We don't usually have much trouble out here, but sometimes kids break in and steal stuff," Kyle said. "It could have been kids from town."

Jolene was considering that when she heard the door open behind her. Her shoulders tensed. She swung around on her stool, ready to confront whoever it was, then relaxed when she recognized Walt, the man she'd met the day before.

"Hey, it's my favorite girl!" Walt said.

Jolene laughed. "Favorite already? We just met."

"Well, anyone who buys me a round is my favorite." Walt chuckled as he slid into the seat next to Jolene and Kyle automatically served him a full shot glass and mug of beer.

Walt downed the shot, coughed and turned to Jolene. "I remembered something else my grandmother told me that you might be interested in."

Jolene's brows rose. "Really? what?"

Walt leaned closer to her. "Seems there was this beautiful woman ... Miss Lily, I think my grandma called her."

Walt paused and his eyes got a faraway look.

"Go on," Jolene prompted.

Walt's eyes sharpened and he looked at her. "Well, Grandma was just a little girl back then and I guess she idolized Miss Lily, you know, like girls do."

Jolene nodded, waiting patiently as he paused to take a sip of beer. "I guess grandma used to try to be like her ... you know, follow her around and such. So, she said one day she'd followed Miss Lily to the coach house where they kept the horses. Grandma snuck in the side and hid behind some bales of hay."

"And?" Jolene's brows shot up as she sipped her beer.

"Lily was arguing with the Sheriff. Grandma thought it was strange they would argue seeing as they were getting married and all." Walt laughed and winked at Jolene. "*We* know that's to be expected when you're married, but Grandma was a little girl with romantic notions."

Jolene noticed that Kyle had his elbows on the bar, leaning forward to hear the story. He snorted. "That's for sure."

Jolene snuck a peek at his ring finger. *Was Kyle married?*

"Anyway," Walt continued, "she said they were arguing about a key and she said it sounded mighty important. The Sheriff said Lily would never find it and that it was buried right in Dead Water."

"A key?" Jolene asked. "What kind of key?"

"Grandma didn't know but she figured it must have been pretty valuable. Said she looked all over Dead Water for this key. She thought it was made of gold."

"Or opened something full of gold, maybe," Jolene suggested.

Walt tilted his head. "Maybe. 'Course she might have heard it wrong or be remembering it all wrong."

Kyle leaned across the bar. His hand brushed against hers sending a spark of electricity up her arm. He reached for her beer mug. "Another beer?"

Jolene frowned at the mug, noticing it was empty already. "Umm ... no, I think one is enough."

Kyle's hand moved from the mug to her wrist, encircling it and making her pulse flutter.

"You don't have to leave, do you?" His gray eyes drilled into hers and Jolene felt like time had stopped. She *did* have to leave. In fact, all her senses were telling her she should leave as fast as she could. So why was she still sitting there, staring at him?

She heard the door behind her swing open, saw Kyle's eyes darken and then felt a heavy arm drape itself across her shoulders.

"So there you are," Jake said, shooting what Jolene took to be a warning glare at Kyle. "Are you ready?"

Kyle straightened and took an interest in rearranging the glasses under the bar.

"Sure, I was just talking to my friend Walt here," Jolene said. "Walt, this is Jake ... Jake, Walt."

The two men shook hands while Jolene pulled some money out of her pocket and tucked it under her empty beer mug.

"Where are you people off to?" Kyle looked from Jolene to Jake.

"I'm taking my little sister to the old mines," Jake answered, taking Jolene's arm and pulling her out of the chair like an overprotective big brother.

Kyle narrowed his eyes at them. "Old mines? What would you want there? That place is dangerous ... and some say haunted."

"Just part of our history research," Jake said. "Plus, I gotta keep Jolene here out of trouble. I would hate to see what might happen to anyone who messes with her."

Kyle's brows shot up and his eyes went wide signaling that he understood Jakes veiled threat. Jolene narrowed her eyes at Jake and wrenched her arm out of his grasp as he walked her to the door.

When they got outside, she turned to face him. "Hey, what's with the big brother act? I can take care of myself, you know."

It was true, she *could* take care of herself, but she had to admit she was touched by Jake's pretense of being her older brother to protect her. It felt good to have someone looking out for her.

"Yeah, I know, I've seen you in action." Jake smiled down at her. "That warning was to protect him more than you—I'd hate to see what might happen to him if he got *you* mad.

Chapter Eight

"So, just where *is* this mine?" Jolene asked as Celeste pulled the Escalade out onto Route 51. The two sisters had opted to drive together in the Cadillac following Luke, Morgan, Fiona and Jake in their other rental, a black Jeep.

"The road to the mines is just past Dead Water and then, I guess, we'll have to figure out which one is number seven." Celeste nodded her head toward the back seat. "The book Dixie lent us is in the back ... there's a picture of Shorty standing in front of the mine so I figured we might be able to figure it out from the picture.

She watched Jolene twist in her seat so she could grab the book, then turned her attention back to the road. They rode in silence while Jolene studied the book, looking at the pictures from all angles. Celeste knew her sister had a photographic memory and figured she was trying to piece together the lay of the land to help them find the mine.

The Jeep took a turn onto a dirt road that led uphill and Celeste followed their cloud of dust, noticing the terrain became more rocky the further they went. Finally they pulled to a stop in front of a big gaping hole carved in the hillside—one of the mines.

"We're here," Celeste announced. Jolene closed the book carefully then put it in the backseat and the sisters jumped out of the car to meet the others.

"This is the opening to one of the mines, but there are several in this area." Jake waved his hand around to indicate the hilly landscape. Celeste slowly turned to take it all in. The ground was sandy but with much more scrub grass than at the hotel or in Dead Water. A few cacti and some trees dotted the landscape. Large rocks lay about, almost as if placed there by giants. She could see three mine entrances from where she stood. Piles of smaller rocks lay in rubble outside them.

The mines weren't anything like she'd pictured. They were just holes in the hillside. The area was overgrown so they looked like natural caves, not something men had dug out in search of gold.

But which one was number seven?

"Which one is Shorty's?" Fiona echoed her thoughts.

"I think it's this one." Jolene pointed at a hole to the left. "Or maybe the one next to it. It's pretty hard to tell from the picture in the book."

Celeste grabbed the book from the car and they tried to compare the landscape behind the picture of Shorty to where they currently were. The problem was, it matched a few of the openings and one hundred years of shrub and tree growth had changed the look of the land.

"I say we pair up and explore each of them," Luke said. "We don't have much time until the sun goes down and we don't want to be out here after dark."

"Jolene and I will take this one," Celeste said pointing to the opening on the left that Jolene had said she'd thought was number seven.

"Okay, Morgan and I will take that one ... and Fiona and Jake, you can take the one over there." Luke pointed to two of the entrances in turn, and then looked at his watch. "Let's meet back here in forty-five minutes."

"Okay." Celeste headed toward her mine with Jolene close behind.

"Now you guys don't do anything in those dark mines that we wouldn't do," Jolene threw over her shoulder at the couples and the two sisters snickered as they disappeared into the dark mouth of the opening.

The cool chill of the mine was a welcome relief from the hot intensity of the sun outside. The dim light, however, was not. Celeste fished the small pen light out of her pocket feeling grateful that Luke had equipped each of them with one before they left.

She shined the light around the mine. "Not much here but blasted out rock."

"What were you expecting? A big number seven or 'Shorty was here' or something?" Jolene teased. "Let's go in further and see what we can see."

Jolene trained her light on the dark tunnel ahead and Celeste followed her in, flashing her light on the walls and floor, hoping to uncover some sort of clue.

About thirty feet in, they came to a split in the tunnel. The sisters stood in the middle, each one shining their light down a different path.

"You wanna stick together or split up?" Jolene asked.

"We can cover more ground if we split up," Celeste answered ignoring the tightening in her stomach that told her it was a bad idea.

"Yeah." Jolene looked at her watch. "We won't go too far in, though. How about we each go ten minutes and then turn back?"

"Sounds good." Celeste held out her fist and the girls did a knuckle tap. Then they disappeared into different tunnels.

The tunnel was more narrow than the main shaft and Celeste took her time picking her way through the small rocks that littered the bottom. The damp, musty smell of earth ticked her nose and she let out a sneeze that echoed loudly in the tunnel. Taking her hand away from her mouth, the beam of her flashlight illuminated something that didn't look quite right on the wall.

She trained the light on the spot. *Was that writing?*

She got close to the wall, squinting at the carvings in the stone. Not writing, but some kind of pictures—like hieroglyphics.

Celeste had no idea what the three symbols carved into the wall meant. Were they put there by some ancient civilization or the miners? If the miners had dug out the tunnel, then it only made sense it was them ... or someone who came here after. It couldn't have been an ancient civilization since the tunnel wouldn't have existed.

She beamed the light up and down the wall on all sides but there were no more symbols. Slowly she walked down the tunnel searching every inch of wall. About five feet down, she found more symbols, then more after another five feet. Curious, she followed the path of symbols deeper into the tunnel.

What did they mean? Celeste had no idea, but she knew someone who did—Cal. She got her cell phone out and snapped a few shots of the symbols. Cal was an expert historian, if anyone could figure out what these were and what they meant, he could. Maybe he would even be able to tear himself away from business and join them, she hoped.

She made her way down the tunnel, taking pictures of all the symbols. She came to another split. Each tunnel had a group of carved symbols on the wall right at the split. She aimed the camera at the symbols on the tunnel wall to the right. The flash in the camera went off as it had before, but this time it illuminated more than just the symbols. She peered into the tunnel letting her eyes adjust after the flash—that couldn't have been …

Her heart jerked when she realized a figure of a man stood just inside the tunnel. Not a flesh and blood man—a ghost … and he didn't look happy.

"What do you think you are doing?" he asked.

Celeste's brows pulled together. He looked familiar. She leaned closer to him, then pulled back realizing who it was—Shorty!

"I'm just exploring." Celeste fought the fear that clutched at her chest.

Shorty had robbed and killed in his lifetime. He hadn't been a nice person and his ghost probably wasn't much different. But his ghost knew where the treasure was—maybe she could get that information out of him if she kept him talking. On the other hand, he might bring her harm. Celeste wasn't sure what kind of harm a ghost could bring, since she'd only encountered friendly ones before, but she didn't want to find out, either. She decided to proceed with caution.

"Get out before you get hurt." Shorty made shooing motions with his hands.

"Is that a threat?" Celeste narrowed her eyes at him and she imagined he looked hurt ... until he took a menacing step toward her, causing her heartbeat to pick up speed.

"Listen girly, you have no business in here." Shorty glanced behind him.

Was something back there he didn't want her to see? The treasure?

"Sure I do," she said boldly. "I need to know what these symbols mean." She aimed the beam of her flashlight on the wall.

Shorty's ghost looked at the wall, his face drawn into a frown. "Symbols?"

Just then, another ghost started to materialize next to Shorty. A woman. The same one Celeste had seen in Dead Water—the one who wanted vindication. Celeste felt a chill. She hoped the ghost wasn't planning to get her revenge right now. The woman looked directly at the symbols illuminated by the flashlight.

"The key is in Dead Water," she said.

"Key? What key?" Shorty and Celeste asked at the same time.

The female ghost opened her mouth to speak, then her eyes widened and she started to fade away as she looked at something behind Celeste.

Celeste turned and saw the ghost of Deke, the old Sheriff of Dead Water. It was like a ghost party in there, how many more would show up?

Deke ignored her and fixed a ghostly glare on Shorty. His feet were planted shoulder length apart and his hands hung at his sides like he was ready for an old Western gunfight. Which Celeste supposed wasn't out of the realm of possibilities as the ghosts were both from the old west and Deke *had* shot Shorty in real life.

"You can't have her, she's mine," Shorty said causing Celeste's stomach to lurch. *Was he talking about her? What was he planning to do to her?*

"Not this time, Shorty." Deke glanced over at Celeste. "You should stay out of this, just like Lily should have."

Celeste didn't know who Lily was but she couldn't agree more. The air in the tunnel was becoming stale with tension and she could hear noises coming from somewhere deep in the mine behind Shorty. It sounded like voices, but distorted with echoes.

More ghosts?

She didn't want to stick around to find out, so she turned and ran.

***

Celeste burst out into the section of tunnel where the two shafts split off, almost knocking over Jolene who had arrived at their meeting spot only seconds before.

"What the heck?" Jolene turned around and grabbed Celeste's arm to keep them both from toppling over. Her eyes narrowed when she looked at Celeste's face. "You look like you just saw a ghost."

Celeste nodded taking a deep breath. "Three, in fact."

Jolene peered into the dark tunnel. "Down there?"

"Yeah." Celeste felt an icy finger run up her spine as she looked back over her shoulder. "This place is giving me the creeps, let's get out of here."

Eager to leave the ghosts behind, Celeste moved forward as quickly as the light from her penlight allowed.

"I also found some markings on the tunnel," Celeste said as they headed toward the mine entrance. "I took pictures of them on my phone."

She pulled one of the pictures up and showed it to Jolene just as the tunnel dumped them out into the fresh air. The sun was setting and Celeste could see Morgan, Luke, Jake and Fiona just coming out of the tunnels they'd explored.

"Did you find something?" Jake nodded toward the phone.

"Some strange markings on the tunnel," Celeste said showing him the screen. "I don't know if they have anything to do with the treasure, but I'm going to send them to Cal and see if he can make heads or tails of them."

"And she saw some ghosts," Jolene said to Jake.

"Oh really?" Jakes eyebrows lifted. "We didn't find anything."

"Neither did we," Luke added. "Just a bunch of rocks and sand. Tell us about the ghosts."

Celeste glanced back at the mine uneasily. "One of them was Shorty. I recognized him from the picture. He didn't seem pleased to see me … told me to get out. I asked him about the markings on the wall but he acted like he didn't even see them. Then she showed up."

"She?" Morgan asked.

"Yeah, the same ghost I saw in Dead Water. She wasn't there long though, because then the Sheriff showed up and scared her away."

"Wait, I thought the sheriff was a good guy," Fiona said.

"He is," Celeste said. "At least I think he is. Not sure why the woman disappeared when he showed up but it seemed like he and Shorty were going to have some kind of fight. He told me to stay out of it and I got a weird feeling so I got out of there as fast as I could."

"That sounds kind of scary." Morgan looked back at the mine opening. "It's good that you listened to your 'weird feeling'. I know mine are always right."

"Yeah, I just wish I could have found something out about the treasure." Celeste pressed her lips together. "Although the woman did say something strange and I wonder if it's some kind of clue."

"What was that?" Luke asked.

"She said something about the key being in Dead Water."

Jolene sucked in a breath and everyone turned to face her.

"Do you know something about a key?" Jake asked.

"No." Jolene's bottom lip caught between her teeth. "It's just that Walt, the old guy in the bar, said when his grandmother was a little girl she overheard one of the ladies in Dead Water and the Sheriff fighting about a key … she said the sheriff told the woman the key was buried in Dead Water and she'd never find it."

"What is the key for?" Fiona asked.

Celeste shrugged. "I have no idea … I don't even know if we can trust her. When I saw her ghost in the cemetery, she said she wanted vindication. So, I wonder—does the key have to do with that or the treasure?"

"Either way, it seems like another trip to Dead Water is in order." Luke narrowed his eyes at something behind Celeste and she turned around to see a cloud of dust approaching them.

"Who's that?" Morgan squinted toward the dust cloud.

"Looks like the police," Jolene said.

Celeste's stomach sank as the brown and black Sheriff's car pulled to a stop. Sheriff Kane didn't seem too happy with them last time and she didn't want another run-in with him. But Kane wasn't driving. Another cop got out. Tall and blond, he wore a Sheriff's Office uniform and a pair of those annoying mirrored sunglasses.

"What are you folks doing here?" Celeste looked at the deputy tag on his shirt thath gave his name— Styles.

"Just taking some scenic pictures, Deputy Styles." Fiona poured on the charm, twirling her red curls.

"Didn't you see the 'No Trespassing' sign?" Apparently, Fiona's charm hadn't worked because Styles was pulling out a pad of pink paper.

"Are you writing a ticket?" Jolene asked.

Styles fixed her with a glare—or at least Celeste thought it was a glare, she couldn't tell with the sunglasses. "Yep. You people know better than to be out here, I think. Didn't Sheriff Kane warn you?"

"Not here. Over at Emma's," Luke answered.

Styles raised a brow and scribbled something on the pad. "This here's a two hundred and fifty dollar fine. Next time I'll throw you in jail."

"What?" Jolene's eyes flashed as Luke calmly took the paper that Styles had ripped from the pad. "That's ridiculous. You can't throw us in jail for trespassing." She glanced at Luke uncertainly. "Can he?"

Luke just shrugged.

Styles whipped off his glasses, his sharp hazel eyes addressed each of them in turn. "I can put you in jail. But listen, it's for your own good. It's not safe around here for more reasons than one. It would be best if you people went on your way and did your historic research in some *other* town."

He shoved the glasses back on, got in his car and sped off.

"Well, what do you make of that?" Fiona stood, hands on hips while she watched the car drive off.

"I get the sneaking suspicion this isn't *just* about trespassing," Morgan said. "There's more to this and I have a gut feeling Deputy Styles wasn't telling us the exact truth."

"Yeah, it's becoming obvious the law doesn't want us here," Jake said.

"And some of the ghosts too," Celeste added.

"Which makes me want to stay and dig into this even more," Luke said. "The way they are acting combined with the break-in makes me think the police—or someone—wants to scare us away from the treasure and if that's the case, it must mean we are getting close."

Chapter Nine

Once they got back to the hotel where there was cell phone service, Celeste sent the pictures of the symbols to Cal.

"Do you think the treasure is in the mine?" Morgan asked as she plucked some of the turkey giblet meat out of the bag and put it on a dish for Belladonna.

"Maybe," Celeste said. "It sure seemed like Shorty was hiding something back there. But I'm not sure I want to go down there ... I heard some ghostly voices."

"Maybe the treasure is haunted." Fiona reached into a bag full of fried chicken that Dave had saved out from the Hotel dinner menu for them.

"Aww, come on," Jake said looking into the bucket and picking out a drumstick. "If you guys fought off those pirates, surely a few ghosts won't scare you."

Celeste laughed at Jake's reference. Earlier that year, they'd had to fight off modern day pirates who were determined to take a treasure that had lain, unbeknownst to them, underneath their home. The pirates were a nasty bunch, but the girls had combined their skills to defeat them. *Could they do the same thing with ghosts?*

"So tomorrow we go to Dead Water and what, exactly, do we look for?" Jolene interrupted Celeste's thoughts.

"The key," Morgan said piling a chicken breast and a roll onto her plate. "Whatever that is."

"It doesn't make much sense." Jolene scrunched her face up. "What's this key open, anyway?"

"Maybe Shorty put the treasure in something that needs a key to open it," Fiona offered.

"Or maybe it's more like a map that shows us which tunnel to take to get to the treasure." Celeste picked at the coleslaw on her plate, glancing anxiously at her phone.

When was Cal going to get back to her?

Before they got together, Cal had been a real ladies man—a confirmed bachelor with a different date every night. She pushed aside a tingle of nervousness that tried to establish itself in her belly. Cal wasn't out with someone else, she was sure of it. He wouldn't do something like that to her ... would he?

"Did anyone find out anything about the new occupant here in the hotel?" Luke asked and Celeste looked up from her cell phone vigil.

"Nope." Everyone shook their heads except Jolene.

"The bartender told me that someone was in the bar asking about us." Jolene shoveled mashed potatoes into her mouth. "I wonder if it was him."

"And if it wasn't, who would be asking about us and why?" Jake asked around a mouthful of chicken.

Celeste's phone chirped with an incoming message and she dove for it. Her heart surged when she saw it was from Cal.

"Cal says the words could be like a code, but you'd need a key to decipher them," Celeste informed the group a few minutes later.

"Like the key we needed for the journal?" Morgan asked, referring to the journal of one of their ancestor's.

The journal they'd found in the attic had eventually led them to the treasure under their house, but it had been written in code and had to be translated. Without Cal knowing what kind of code it was and how to find the translation cypher, they never would have found the treasure.

"Yeah." Celeste smiled down at the phone, her stomach fluttering. "He said he's coming out to meet us here tomorrow night."

"And you have that big smile plastered on your face because you're happy he can help us decode the symbols?" Fiona's teasing remark caused Celeste's cheeks to warm.

"Of course." Celeste plastered a wide-eyed innocent look on her face.

Morgan and Fiona snickered.

"I'm going to do some more research on the treasure and see if I can get a lead on this key." Jolene dumped her paper plate in the trash, then got behind the desk and tapped on the computer. "It might help us to know exactly what we're looking for."

Celeste threw out her own plate and settled onto the micro-suede couch noticing it was a lot more comfortable than the old one. Belladonna jumped up onto the end table beside her, knocking the book Dixie had lent them into her lap.

"Oh, I guess I can flip through here and see if I find anything useful." Celeste opened the book, looking at the table of contents. Belladonna reached a velvety paw out and touched the page.

"Careful, Belladonna. This book is on loan." Celeste gently pushed the cat's paw aside but Belladonna just put it right back on the book, this time lifting the edge of the pages with a finely honed claw.

"Cut it out, I don't want the pages to get ripped." Celeste picked the cat up and put her on the floor.

"Meow!" Belladonna jumped back up onto the couch swishing her tail in Celeste's face. Celeste took her hands off the book to push the fluffy white tail aside. Belladonna shot her paw out to the pages of the book, flipping some over to a section of old pictures.

"Hey, I said—"

Celeste stared down at the page in the book, her words catching in her throat. Sitting in the middle of the page was a picture of the ghost Celeste had seen in the mine and at Dead Water. She wore a fancy dress, her hair piled high on her head. Underneath the caption read, 'Lily Sweetwater'.

Where had she heard that name before?

"Is something the matter?" Morgan asked.

Celeste looked up at her sister. "I think I just found our lady ghost."

"Really?"

Celeste held the book up and pointed at the picture. "It says her name was Lily Sweetwater."

"Maybe we should Google her and see if that leads us to any clues," Fiona said, glancing over at Jolene.

"Did you say Lily?" Jolene's forehead creased.

"Yep. Sweetwater."

"Remember how I told you about the old-timer in the bar and how his grandma followed a lady around? The lady fought with the Sheriff about some key," Jolene said.

"Yes," Celeste replied.

"Well, that lady's name was Lily," Jolene said. "And I think he said she was married to the Sheriff."

"Deke?"

Jolene shrugged. "I guess so. He never said the Sheriff's name."

"Well this all can't be coincidence," Morgan said. "I have a feeling it all ties together somehow."

"But how?" Luke asked.

"I don't know, but I think we're on the right track," Morgan answered. "Maybe there is more about her in the book or online."

"Meow."

Celeste reached over to pat Belladonna. "Looks like Belladonna inadvertently gave us a clue by flipping to the page with the picture."

"Maybe it wasn't inadvertent." Fiona wiggled her eyes at Celeste.

"Yeah." Jake laughed. "Too bad the cat doesn't have some secret knowledge and can tell us where the treasure is. Then we could avoid all this clue chasing."

Luke joined in the laughter and the two men shook their heads.

Celeste looked over at the cat. It *did* seem kind of strange that she was always turning up clues for them.

Did she have some secret knowledge?

Celeste bent down to study the cat closer. Belladonna slid her eyes over to look at Celeste, then blinked, curled into a ball and went to sleep.

Shaking her head, Celeste turned her attention to the book. Lily's story was the typical Cinderella story of a beautiful woman that came out west, worked as a saloon girl and then married the Sheriff. The Sheriff died mysteriously two weeks after their wedding. A picture of the wedding showed a grim faced Lily with Deke in his sheriff outfit at her side.

"Boy, Lily doesn't look too happy in her wedding picture." Celeste flashed the picture around the room.

"Walt's grandma heard them fighting in the stable, maybe they were fighting at their wedding too." Jolene said.

"Maybe," Celeste said flipping to the next chapter. "Oh, here it talks about the stagecoach robberies. Maybe we'll find something of interest."

She read quickly, skipping over the boring stuff and picking out the parts that might be important to their search.

"It says the stagecoaches were robbed by a lone masked man. It was a mystery how he knew when the coach was coming because it came at all different times."

"Interesting. How many robberies were there?" Jolene asked.

"Five all together." Celeste's fingers scanned the page, picking out the important stuff. "It says he made off with silver and gold and also jewelry he stole from any passengers that were unlucky enough to be traveling on the coach. Looks like he struck pay dirt with one necklace he ripped right off the neck of a Mrs. Simon Brandt—the Vanderbeek necklace—it was worth one hundred twenty thousand even back then!"

Celeste stared down at a picture of the opulent necklace. Even in black and white, she could see the exquisite beauty of the diamond-studded collar. It was covered in stones with teardrop shaped rubies and emeralds hanging down like a waterfall. "The necklace has never been seen since."

Jolene's fingers tapped the keys of her computer. "That necklace alone is worth two point eight million today."

"Wow. Combine that with the value of the gold and silver reputed to have been stolen in the robberies and the treasure is worth about four million," Fiona said.

Jake whistled. "Not to mention all the other jewelry and valuables that might have been stolen from the passengers."

Celeste nodded. "Deke must have figured out it was Shorty somehow, and he must have been right because the robberies stopped after he shot him."

"Walt told me about some love triangle scandal back then. Maybe Deke, Shorty and Lily were the love triangle and that's why she looks unhappy at the wedding," Jolene said.

"Or maybe Shorty wanted the beautiful saloon girl and Deke saved her from Shorty's clutches and stopped the stagecoach robberies at the same time by shooting him," Luke added.

"And then Lily married her hero, Deke, who tragically died weeks later." Fiona sighed. "What a romantic story."

Celeste laughed. "You might not be too far off. When I was in the mine with the ghosts, Shorty said *you can't have her, she's mine*. I thought they were actually talking about me at the time and was scared Shorty's ghost was planning on doing something to me."

"But he *could* have been talking about Lily," Morgan said.

"I guess so." Celeste's eyes narrowed—she remembered where she'd heard the name "Lily" before. "And then Deke said something strange. He said something like 'You should stay out of this just like Lily should have'."

"What's that mean? Stay out of what?" Jolene asked.

Celeste shrugged. "That, I have no idea about."

"Maybe she found out some secret and that's why they argued," Jolene said.

"Or maybe it wasn't even Deke she argued with," Morgan replied. "How reliable is that story, anyway?"

Jolene pressed her lips together. "Good question. I got it second hand from an old-timer who heard it from his grandmother years after it actually happened. Maybe it's not even true."

"Hopefully when we go to Dead Water tomorrow Lily will grace Celeste with her appearance and fill us in," Luke said.

"I don't know," Celeste replied, a hollow feeling in her chest. "She seemed like a shy, reluctant ghost."

"But you've already seen her twice, so at least there's some hope," Fiona reminded her.

"Yeah, maybe if we give her what she wants, I can get her to talk," Celeste said.

"What does she want?" Jake asked.

"Vindication," Celeste answered. "Or at least that's what she said when we saw her in the cemetery."

"Vindication for what?" Luke's forehead pleated as he looked at her.

"I'm not sure." Celeste flipped to the table of contents in the book. "I'll have to look through here and see what it is she could be referring to."

"I think it's important to find out." Morgan's ice-blue eyes sparkled with excitement. "Because something tells me that whatever it is has something to do with Shorty Hanson and the hidden treasure."

Chapter Ten

"This place is so cool!" Jolene stood in the middle of the street, in the center of Dead Water, her brown leather cowboy boots stirring up sand as she turned to look at every part of the ghost town.

Celeste smiled at the look of wonder on her sister's face. The place *was* pretty cool—all that history and the old buildings still almost intact. She couldn't wait to show it to Cal.

"Okay, let's get to work," Luke said. "I figure we can split up and search the buildings. Look for any hiding spots, like hidden compartments in walls."

"And look on the outside too," Jake added, "False bricks or stones can be good for hiding stuff."

"So should we all take a building, then?" Morgan asked.

"Sure, but if you go inside just be careful—the floors might not be safe."

Jolene, Fiona, Morgan, Luke and Jake each chose the building they wanted and then walked off leaving Celeste alone in the center of town. She'd picked the saloon since that's where she had seen Lily's ghost before. As she walked over to the entrance, she chewed on her bottom lip anxiously—

she knew they were counting on her talking to Lily about the key but she couldn't just conjure up a ghost. Ghosts usually came to *her*, she didn't have any control over when ... or if ... one would show up.

The building creaked ominously when she entered, as if the ghosts of the past were trying to warn her away. She walked over to the far end, where the stairway lay in a pile on the floor. Squatting down, she ran her hand along what was left of the old banister. The smooth wood felt like satin under her fingers. She closed her eyes and imagined herself walking down the stairs, dressed in a long gown, her blond hair piled on her head. The sounds of clinking glasses and conversation floating up to her from the saloon below as she descended.

"It was a nice place in its time."

Celeste's eyes flew open and she jerked her hand back. The misty ghost of Lily swirled in front of her.

"I'm sure it was." Celeste stood up.

Lily sighed. "It was good here, until everything went wrong."

"What went wrong? Do you mean the stagecoach robberies?"

"That's just part of it." Lily turned and walked to the bar. Celeste followed.

"What else happened?" Celeste asked.

"Betrayal, a cover up ..." Lily looked down and put her hand on her stomach. Celeste's heart skipped a beat when she noticed a pink ring on Lily's finger—the same ring they'd dug up over at Emma's. "I did what I had to do."

"What did you have to do?" Celeste's brows knit together.

What had Lily done?

Lily looked afraid, her ghost started to fade out. Panic clutched at Celeste's chest—she was going to lose her one chance to find out about the key.

"What do you want vindication for?" Celeste blurted out the words and Lily's ghost swirled, coming in a little clearer like an old-fashioned television picture that had been fine-tuned.

"It's not for me," she said.

"Then who? Maybe we can help ... if you'll help us figure out where the key is." Celeste held her breath for Lily's answer.

"It's all in the letters," Lily said.

"Letters? What letters?"

"Emma has the letters," Lily said, her ghost starting to evaporate.

"Wait!" Celeste begged. "What about the key?"

Lily's voice was barely a whisper. "You'll find out everything in the letters—only after the truth is read will I show you where the key is."

***

Celeste exited the saloon and looked down the street. She could see Fiona and Morgan inspecting the bottom corner of what used to be the general store. Luke was at the end of the street near a brick structure and Jake was just coming out of the Sheriff's office.

As Celeste started toward Fiona and Morgan, Jolene came out of the next building.

"Did you find anything?" Celeste squinted at her younger sister.

"Nothing but old dust and some splinters," Jolene said frowning down at her fingertips.

As they approached Fiona and Morgan, the two older sisters stood up from where they'd been squatting near the corner of the general store.

"Did you find something?" Jolene asked.

Fiona shook her head. "Nothing. We thought there might be a secret hiding place, but it was just filled with cobwebs."

Celeste heard the scuff of boots behind her and turned to see Luke and Jake.

"Did you all come up empty?" Luke asked, and then turned to Celeste. "Even you?"

"No, actually I think I got us another lead." Celeste smiled. "I saw Lily's ghost in the saloon."

Luke's brows shot up. "And?"

Celeste told them about the deal she'd made with Lily.

"So we need to get these letters from Emma?" Jake asked. "What makes you think she'd give them to you?"

"Well, I'm not sure she will, but it's worth a try," Celeste said. "There must be some kind of connection between Lily and Emma and I think we have something that might help persuade her to entrust us with the letters."

"What's that?"

"The ring with the pink stone we dug up the other day. Lily's ghost was wearing one just like it."

Chapter Eleven

Emma's trailer was located about a half mile off route 51. Her driveway, if you could call it that, was a dirt road that meandered through the desert on the edge of the property they'd previously searched with the metal detectors.

Nerves fluttered in Celeste's stomach as they approached the trailer. She had no idea if they'd be welcomed or chased off with a shotgun.

The trailer itself, although decades old, was kept in good repair. In the front, wood-sided raised garden beds held rich loam that fed the lush herbs and flowers Emma had miraculously managed to grow under the desert sun. Vintage metal patio chairs, their fresh turquoise paint gleaming in the sun, sat under an awning that extended from the side of the trailer.

Morgan rapped her knuckles on the metal door and the hollow, tinny sound elicited a chorus of barks from inside. Celeste saw Fiona's face crease with worry and she knew her sister was thinking the same thing. Hopefully Emma wouldn't have her dogs chase them off.

The door opened and Emma's keen blue eyes squinted out at them. A reddish-brown hound dog on either side of her pushed to get out, sniffing and snapping. Emma shushed them and they quieted down with a whimper.

"You're the treasure hunters, aren't you?" she asked.

"Yes, that's right," Morgan said. "We met the other day."

Emma nodded. "I remember, I'm not senile you know. Why are you here?"

"We wanted to give you this." Fiona held out the ring they'd dug up. Emma pushed her face out the door. Her brows mashed together, then widened as her face softened.

"My great-grandmother's ring." Emma opened the door wider and reached out. Fiona dropped the ring into her hand. Emma smiled as she held it up in front of her face.

"We dug it up the other night, but with the excitement and the Sheriff coming and all, I forgot all about it until I found it in my jeans pocket this morning." Celeste saw Fiona cross her fingers behind her back as she told the little white lie. "We figured you'd want it so we hurried over with it."

"Of course." Emma pushed the door wide and the two hounds rushed out sniffing enthusiastically at their feet. "Where are my manners? Would you girls like some lemonade?"

"We'd love some." Morgan answered for all of them as she bent to pet one of the dogs.

"These are my dogs, Clive and Lucy," Emma said. "They must like you girls. Otherwise they'd be barking and trying to chase you off."

Celeste's shoulders relaxed with relief. If the dogs liked them, then chances were Emma would too. And the offer of lemonade was promising.

Emma pointed at the patio chairs. "Just have a seat and I'll be right out with the lemonade. I made it fresh this morning."

The girls sat down while Clive and Lucy divided their attention between them. They seemed to favor Morgan and Jolene, which was no surprise since both girls had a way with animals.

"You're a good dog," Morgan said as she cupped Clive's face in her hands. "I can tell these dogs are very loyal to Emma."

"Yes, they are," Emma said as she came up behind them, balancing a large tray that held a pitcher and glasses in her hand. "How did you know?

Morgan shrugged. "I just know things sometimes."

Emma looked at her strangely as she set the tray down. The ice cubes clinked together as she picked up the pitcher and poured lemon-colored liquid into the glasses, which she handed to the girls.

"Clive and Lucy never leave my side. I have to lock them in the trailer if I want to go out without them. I did that the other night when I confronted you, since I was afraid they might get overprotective of me and I didn't want them to harm you."

The dogs sat on either side of Emma as if to prove her right.

"So, where are your men?" Emma asked.

Celeste had to think for a minute before she realized Emma meant Luke and Jake. The guys had begged off accompanying them saying they wanted to look into the break-in and try to talk to the mystery guest at the hotel. Everyone agreed that Emma might be better persuaded to reveal the letters if it was just the girls, anyway, and it looked like their instincts were right.

"Oh, they're off doing guy stuff," Fiona said. "We wanted to get you the ring as soon as possible so we came without them."

"Did you say it was your great-grandmothers?" Morgan asked.

"Yes." Emma looked at the ring that she'd slipped on her finger. "I never saw it in person, but grandma had some pictures of her mother—my great-grandmother—with it on. It was special to her, I guess."

"Oh why is that?" Jolene cocked her head to one side as she looked at the ring on Emma's finger.

"I don't rightly know." Emma pressed her lips together. "Grandma used to tell me lots of stories about the old days and her Ma. She didn't have any Pa—I guess he'd passed on before she was born."

"And you're family always lived on this land?" Celeste's brow creased as she looked around. The trailer was only about thirty years old and there was no other house in sight.

"Oh no," Emma said. "We lived just outside of Couver City."

"But didn't you say this land had been in your family since the 1800s?" Celeste asked.

"Yes." Emma nodded as she sipped her lemonade. "It has, but no one lived here for decades. When I got to be in my forties I had a hankerin' to move away from it all and live a simple life. Alone. So, since my family already owned the land outright, I bought this trailer and put it here."

"Shorty Hanson lived here in the gold mining days, back when Dead Water was a thriving town, didn't he?"

Emma nodded. "Everyone thinks he buried a treasure here and many have come to dig it up ... just like you girls did."

"But you don't think he did?"

Emma shook her head. "No. Family legend has it that he didn't rob those stagecoaches ... someone else did it and framed him. Only a few people in the town back then believed him though, and ... well, the rest is history."

"So, you must be related to him, then?"

"Well I guess I must." Emma's brow wrinkled. "I'm not sure, though. I actually don't think I am ... seems he left the land to my great-grandma for some reason."

"The one that had the ring?" Morgan asked.

Emma looked down at the ring, her brow still wrinkled. "Yes, I guess so. She was married to the Sheriff in Dead Water, so I guess I must be a descendant of his—I hope he was a nicer Sheriff than Sheriff Kane."

"Her name was Lily Sweetwater," Celeste said.

Emma jerked her head toward Celeste. "That's right! How did you know?"

Celeste cleared her throat and the sisters exchanged an uneasy look. "I saw her."

Emma laughed. "Don't be silly, she's been dead for almost eighty years."

"She's not joking," Morgan said.

Emma turned her steely gaze on Celeste. "That's impossible."

"I really did see her. Or I should say I saw her ghost."

"I don't believe in ghosts," Emma said.

Celeste puffed out her cheeks. "Well, I hope you won't think I'm crazy, but Lily told me about some letters from back then she wants us to read. She seems to think they will reveal something that happened in the 1870s ... something she feels needs some kind of vindication."

"Vindication? For what?" Emma asked.

"I don't know." Celeste gave Emma her most trustworthy look. "But if it has something to do with your ancestors, then I'd think you'd want that to come to light."

Emma stared at her for a few seconds, and then she looked down, her bottom lip catching between her teeth. "Seems I do recall an old set of letters. Ma found them after grandma passed. I never read them, but they looked old. They've been sitting in a drawer with some other old family things ever since."

"It would mean a lot to us if we could see them." Celeste perched on the edge of her seat, her muscles taut with tension.

Emma stared at her, and then looked at each of her sisters. She nodded slowly and stood. "All right. I consider myself to be a good judge of character and I think you girls are okay. I'll let you look at them, but I want them back."

Celeste relaxed back into her chair. "I really appreciate that. Of course, we'll return them in perfect condition."

Emma went inside and the girls breathed a collective sigh of relief. Clive and Lucy stood guard at the door of the trailer until Emma came out, a pile of yellowed papers tied with a faded red ribbon in her hand.

"Here they are. Still tied with the old ribbon." Emma handed the package to Celeste then started rounding up the empty lemonade glasses.

Celeste took the last sip from her glass. The drink was perfectly sweetened with just a hint of tartness from the lemon. A mint leaf enhanced the flavor. Celeste pulled the leaf out of the glass and chewed on it.

"That's mint from my garden." Emma tilted her chin toward the raised garden bed full of herbs as she balanced the glass on the tray.

"I noticed your gardens," Morgan said. "It's a miracle you can get stuff to grow in this climate."

Emma laughed. "A lot of water and good loam helps. My family's been into growing herbs since I can remember. In fact, they tell me my great-grandma, Lily was quite the herbalist."

"She must have been if she could grow stuff out here in the 1870s," Morgan said. "I'm an herbalist myself."

"Is that so?" Emma asked as she moved toward the trailer. "Well, maybe someday we can trade tips."

"I'd like that," Morgan said as she stood. "Well, I guess we should be going."

Emma opened the trailer door and put the lemonade tray down on something just inside.

"Well, it was nice of you girls to come by and I do appreciate you giving me the ring." She looked down at her finger again. "Less honest folk would have just taken it and I never would have known."

"We would never do that," Celeste said.

"I know that now," Emma said. "And I enjoyed the company. Feel free to come back anytime you want."

"Thanks." Celeste held up the packet of letters. "And thanks for letting us read these. I'll get them back to you within the next couple of days."

"Now, you girls be careful. I heard you had some trouble at the hotel." Emma leaned down to pet Lucy's head.

"The break-in?" Celeste asked.

Emma nodded. "If you ask me, that Sheriff Kane is behind it. He seemed like he didn't want you folks hanging around here."

"You can say that again," Jolene said. "His deputy threatened to throw us in jail the other day."

"He did? On what grounds?" Emma asked.

"We were out at the mines exploring, and he drove right up and gave us a big old fine," Jolene answered. "He said if he caught us there again he'd throw us in jail."

Emma's eyes narrowed. "Is that so? You know years ago, no one cared if people explored there. But ever since Kane became Sheriff, they've been real touchy about anyone going up there."

"Why?" Morgan asked.

Emma's gaze drifted over to the mines about a mile away across bare flat land. She had a clear view of them from her property. "I'm not sure, but I'd bet my eye teeth something funny is going on up there ... At night sometimes, I see things and hear things and it ain't just my age."

The sister's exchanged a look. Emma seemed sharp as a tack. Celeste doubted she was seeing or hearing things that weren't there. She remembered how Sheriff Kane had seemed eager to get Emma off her property and into the city. But why?

"Of course, the sheriff and others in town would have you believe that the mines are haunted but, as I said, I don't believe in ghosts. I think he just says that to keep people away," Emma added.

"What could be going on up there that the Sheriff wouldn't want anyone to know about?" Fiona asked.

"I don't know, but I plan to find out," Emma said as she stroked the dog's ears absently. "... And sooner rather than later."

***

Celeste's fingers rasped on the dry paper of the letters as Morgan pulled the Escalade out onto Route 51. She fingered the silky ribbon as she looked down at the barely discernible faded blue writing.

What secrets did the letters hold?

She was dying to read them and had all she could do to not rip them open in the back of the car —the only thing that held her back was she didn't want them to get damaged. Better to wait until they were back at the hotel where she could place them out on a clean surface and read them in an orderly manner.

Besides, her excitement to pick up Cal at the airport—where they were now heading—trumped her excitement to read the letters, so she kept them safe in her lap.

"Do you guys think Sheriff Kane is up to something, like Emma says?" Jolene twisted in the passenger seat to look at Celeste and Fiona in the back.

"Sure seems that way," Fiona said. "He's probably after the treasure, just like us."

"And that deputy must be in on it too," Jolene added.

"Maybe even the whole police force," Morgan said.

Celeste pressed her lips together. "If he is, then he must have information the treasure is in one of the gold mines, so we're on the right track. Otherwise he wouldn't be protecting that area the way he is."

"What if Kane already knows where it is?" Jolene asked.

"I don't think he does." Fiona narrowed her eyes. "Because he'd already have taken it out, right? He must still be looking or he wouldn't be trying to scare people off."

"Unless there's more to it than just a cache of treasure," Morgan said as she signaled to turn into the entrance of the small airport where Cal's plane was scheduled to land.

"Maybe there's a vein of gold still active in the mine," Jolene suggested.

"Whatever it is, it might make sense to follow the Sheriff. He could lead us straight to the treasure and we wouldn't have to worry about old letters and cryptic keys," Fiona said.

"That's not a bad idea." Morgan pulled to a stop at the passenger loading area outside the airport and pulled her cell phone out of her purse. "I'll call Luke and see if he can have Buzz and Gordy put a tail on our friendly law enforcement."

Celeste was already opening her door. She could see Cal, just inside the glass entrance to the airport. She resisted the urge to run to him and walked over to the door. The smile that lit Cal's face when he saw her from the other side of the glass made her stomach do somersaults.

He burst out of the door and folded her into his arms right before making her knees weak with a smoldering kiss.

"Ahem ..."

Celeste grudgingly broke the kiss and turned to Jolene who was standing beside them, hands on hips, with a disgusted look on her face.

"You have luggage?" She raised her brows at Cal who nodded. "Then let's get it and go."

Cal laughed as she pivoted on her heel in mock disgust and headed toward the luggage claim where his bag was already spinning around the carousel.

He grabbed it, shoved it in the hatch of the Escalade and, after greeting all the sisters, settled into the back seat next to Celeste.

"Somebody fill me in on what's been going on," he said.

Between the four of them, the girls brought him up to speed on the events since they'd come to Nevada ending with the story of the trip out to Emma's to get the letters.

"Do you have more pictures of the symbols from the mine?" he asked after carefully inspecting the brittle pack of letters.

Celeste pulled up the pictures on her cell phone and handed it to Cal so he could scroll through them himself.

He spent several minutes studying them, pressing his lips together and nodding as he scrolled.

"Yeah, these look like some sort of coded symbols." He handed the phone back to Celeste. "But they are meaningless without the chart to decode them."

"Like a key, right?" Jolene asked. "Walt specifically used the word 'key' and so did Lily's ghost."

"You could call it a key, sure," Cal replied.

"Do you think they could mark the path to the treasure?" Fiona leaned across Celeste to look at Cal. "They run down both passages ... and who knows how many after that so we don't know which tunnel to take. We don't even know how many tunnels there are off the main shafts. One could easily get lost in there."

"They could mark the path to a treasure, but they could also be for something else." Cal shrugged. "They could indicate where the veins of gold were ... they could be markings that kept the miners from getting lost inside the tunnels, or they could just be the old miner's version of graffiti."

Celeste felt her stomach sink. What if the markings didn't have anything to do with the treasure and this was all a wild goose chase?

"I'd like to get a look at them in person. Maybe that will tell me more." Cal looked out at the setting sun. "But it's getting dark so I guess we'll have to save that for tomorrow—after I spend tonight getting reacquainted with Celeste."

Jolene groaned and rolled her eyes at them before twisting around to face front. Fiona made gagging noises next to Celeste.

Cal laughed at the sisters' antics but Celeste couldn't help the warm tingle of anticipation that spread through her. And judging by the look in Cal's sapphire eyes, he was feeling the same way.

Chapter Twelve

"They have the best breakfasts here at the hotel. I know you're going to love them," Celeste said to Cal as she stood poised at the top of the steps outside their suite.

"Good because I'm starving." Cal came out the door with Jolene, Morgan and Luke following behind him.

Celeste started down the stairs. At the bottom, she could see the sun streaming through the double oak doors that led outside. A man opened the left door and Celeste's memory tingled. He looked familiar but she couldn't see clearly—the glare of the sun put him in shadow. His thick, dark wavy hair reminded her of the mysterious man, Mateo, who had helped them get the final clue they needed on their last treasure hunt. But, it couldn't be … what would *he* be doing here? And if it was him, *why* would he avoid them?

"Hey, hold on!" Luke pushed his way past her practically knocking her down the stairs. He sprinted across the lobby and out the door. Celeste looked back at Morgan who shrugged.

The four of them continued down the stairs and were turning toward the dining room when Luke came back in.

"What was that about?" Morgan asked.

"I thought that might be the other guest. We still haven't been able to question him." Luke pressed his lips together. "But I missed him. He was in his car and pulling out onto the road before I even got out the door."

Morgan narrowed her eyes at the door. She opened her mouth to say something but was interrupted by Dixie behind her.

"I hope you folks weren't coming down for breakfast."

Celeste turned to Dixie who looked like she was about to cry. "Why, what's wrong?"

"Sheriff Kane shut down the kitchen." Dixie's lower lip trembled.

Morgan's brows knit together. "What? Why?"

A tear slipped out of the corner of Dixie's eye and she covered her face. Morgan rushed to her side, putting her arm around the woman's shoulders, and leading her into the empty dining room.

Dixie collapsed into a chair, her shoulders shaking. "A big chunk of our income comes from the dining." She sobbed. "I'll be out of business in no time. Who's going to stay at a hotel with no meals?"

Celeste's heart ached for Dixie as she sat on her left side, rubbing Dixie's arm through the crisp, white long sleeved blouse and making soothing noises. Morgan sat on Dixie's right, echoing Celeste. Luke, Cal and Jolene pulled out chairs on the other side of the table.

After a minute, Dixie stopped crying.

"Sorry, I'm not usually emotional like this," she sniffed, "but my grandmother said the hotel was so important to her parents—the ones that built it—and I wanted so badly to restore it and keep it running just like they did to honor their memory."

"Why did he close down the kitchen? Did he find some violation or something?" Jolene asked.

Dixie shook her head. "He said he it didn't pass the cleanliness inspection but I'm sure he made that up."

Celeste remembered how spotless the kitchen was when they'd gone in there the day before. "I'm sure he must have. But why? Maybe it was just a mistake?"

Dixie shook her head. "It's no mistake. He means to put me under. For some reason he's been doing everything he can to make me go out of business."

"Does he have a grudge against you or something?" Cal asked.

"No, I don't even know him." Dixie blew her nose on a napkin. "But ever since he became sheriff, it seems he's been trying to shut me down."

The five of them exchanged a glance and Celeste knew what the others were thinking. *Did this have something to do with what was going on out at the mine?*

"But I shouldn't be burdening you folks with my problems." Dixie waved them away. "I'll make do, somehow."

"But the hotel ... can you do something to get the kitchen opened again?" Celeste asked.

"I don't know. I'll talk to my attorney but it seems that Sheriff Kane's influence reaches far." Dixie straightened and her face turned cold. "But I won't give up ... I plan to fight for what's rightfully mine. Our family's had enough stolen from it—I won't let that happen to the hotel too."

Dixie shook her head and put her hand on Morgan and Celeste's arms. "Thanks for listening to me—I just hope the kitchen shutdown doesn't inconvenience you, I know you like to take your meals here."

"Oh, don't worry about that," Morgan said. "We'll miss Dave's cooking, but we can fend for ourselves."

Dixie stood up and then leaned over the table, lowering her voice to a whisper. "We still have the kitchen *and* the food so if you get really hungry just let me know and I can have Dave whip something up for you." She winked at them. "It will be our little secret."

Celeste felt her heart sinking as she watched Dixie walk away. "We can't just sit by and let the hotel go out of business or get closed down."

Cal's deep blue eyes scanned the room taking in the carved wood molding, stained glass windows and period architecture. "It sure would be a shame. This place is really nice down here. Much nicer than our rooms. I'd love to see it get restored."

"I can't imagine why the Sheriff would want to put her out of business," Jolene said.

"If it's not a personal grudge then maybe he wants the land," Morgan replied. "Maybe he wants to build a strip mall or something."

Celeste cringed, thinking of a strip mall standing here instead of the beautiful hotel. "Maybe we can invest in the hotel or something to help her out?"

"I doubt she'd take our money. She seems too proud." Morgan glanced at the door Dixie had disappeared through. "What did she mean when she said her family had had enough stolen from it already?"

Celeste shrugged. "I have no idea ... probably old family history. There might be something about that in the book on Dead Water she lent us."

"Maybe I can have my attorney look into this rezoning and the kitchen shut down," Cal said. "She's pretty good. If something isn't on the up and up she might be able to get them to back off."

"In the meantime, we need to start reading through those letters and find out what Lily wanted vindication for so we can get her to show us the key," Celeste said.

"Yeah, and I'd like to get out to the mine and see Dead Water ... I still have a lot of questions about the treasure," Cal added.

"And I have the most important question of all." Jolene pushed her chair back from the table and stood.

"What's that?" Morgan asked.

"What are we going to eat for breakfast?"

Chapter Thirteen

After rousing Fiona and Jake from their room and telling them about the kitchen shutdown, they voted to go to a diner in Couver City for breakfast. Celeste nibbled on a waffle while she sat patiently watching the rest of them devour bacon, eggs and coffee, wondering if she was the only one anxious to get to the letters.

Once finished, they prolonged her agony by insisting on showing Cal the ghost town of Dead Water and then taking him to see the markings in the mine. Thankfully, they didn't go far into the mine—apparently, Cal saw what he needed after only venturing as far in as Celeste had.

"None of the other mine shafts have markings?" Cal asked as they emerged into the sunlight.

"Nope," Celeste answered. "We checked all the ones around here. But there might be other entrances we don't know about."

She glanced around the area trying to make out any unusual outcroppings or indents that might be other entrances. As she made her survey, she noticed a cloud of dust off in the distance. Another car.

Was it following them?

"Who's that?" She pointed to the cloud and the rest of them turned their heads in that direction.

Fiona shaded her eyes from the sun. "I can't tell. Are they coming or going?"

"Crap, I hope it's not that deputy again." Jolene squinted toward the cloud. "I don't want to get thrown in jail."

"Don't worry. I think it's moving away from us." Luke's eyes turned hard as he stared at the cloud. "But that reminds me—I should check in with Buzz and Gordy and see how their surveillance of the Sheriff is going."

"And I need to check my messages and see if my attorney found out anything about the rezoning," Cal said.

"And I need to get back to the hotel and dig into those letters so we can find out what Lily wanted vindication for, get the key to those symbols and recover the treasure." A note of exasperation crept into Celeste's voice. "You know—the whole reason why we are here in the first place."

Everyone stared at her. They were used to her being on an even keel. Cal laughed and slid his arms around her shoulders.

"Of course, we should get on that right away," he said leading the way toward the cars.

Luke and Jake knew their skills were better put to use trying to figure out what Sheriff Kane was up to and trying to hunt down the mysterious hotel guest, so they dropped Celeste, Cal, Fiona, Morgan and Jolene off at the hotel.

"This will be easier if we spread the letters out on the table in the kitchenette," Morgan suggested. "I'll clean it off."

Celeste carefully pulled the packet of letters out of the bureau drawer in her room and brought them out to the kitchen. Sitting on one of the chairs at the table, she gingerly slipped the ribbon off the packet.

A swirl spiraled up in front of her as the ribbon came off and Celeste felt a stab of excitement. Was Lily's ghost going to materialize and help them? Her excitement deflated as fast as it came when the swirl fell to the table in a pile of decades old dust.

"There are a lot of letters here," Celeste said spreading them out on the table and counting. "Twenty-one, to be exact."

Fiona flicked at the corner of one with a red tipped fingernail. "They're very brittle. We need to be careful handling these."

"Where should we start?" Morgan asked.

Celeste's teeth worried her bottom lip. "I'm not sure. I think we need to read them chronologically."

"I hope they're dated," Jolene said, bending over Morgan's shoulder to look at the table.

Celeste picked through the yellowed papers. They were covered with the faded blue writing of an early fountain pen—so faded that they could barely be seen in some spots. She managed to pick out a few with dates and set them aside in order.

"I guess we'll start with this one." She picked a letter out of the pile, her heart beat quickening at the prospect of looking into a bit of history and solving the mystery of whatever Lily wanted vindicated.

The letter was folded in thirds and she opened it slowly, holding her breath as she spread it flat on the table, praying that it wouldn't rip at the folds.

Belladonna jumped up into her lap with a quiet "mew" as she bent over the table, trying to decipher the old handwriting.

Fiona, Morgan, Jolene and Cal were doing the same. Celeste could barely make out the words. Her eyes scanned the letter—it was signed by Lily, of course. Her eyes drifted back up to the top to find out who Lily had written the letter *to*.

Fiona's sharp intake of breath told Celeste that she'd seen the same thing and their eyes met over the table. Celeste looked up at the others.

"This letter is from Lily to Shorty."

"What?" Morgan narrowed her eyes and bent closer to the letter. "Well I'll be ... and she calls him 'My dearest Shorty'. What's up with that?"

Celeste shrugged. "I guess we need to read them to find out."

Celeste focused on the first two letters. They were formal, much more than a letter today would be, but there was no mistaking the emotion in them.

"These sound like love letters," Morgan said.

"If they are, they're kind of lame," Jolene answered.

"That's how they wrote back then. Everything was more formal, they didn't use explicit words like you young kids do today." Cal teased Jolene.

"I think they're beautiful." Fiona pointed to a passage in one of the letters.

The kiss you stole under the tree
You didn't have to steal from me.

Jolene made a face. "Blech, that's too lovey-dovey." She yawned and her back cracked as she stretched. "This is boring. When do we get to find out about the key?"

"It could take a while ... we need to look these over carefully." Celeste flipped one of the letters over gingerly taking care not to bend it for fear it would rip. "Whatever Lily wanted vindication for might not be obvious so it could take time for us to figure it out."

"Yeah, you're probably right." Jolene let out a sigh and paced around the room.

Morgan looked at her watch. "It's almost three thirty. Maybe you could go do some grocery shopping."

"Yeah, the kitchen's closed here so I guess we might as well cook." Fiona cast an uncertain glance at the stove. "Does that thing even work?"

Jolene went over to the stove and turned one of the knobs. The pilot clicked a few times and then a whooshing sound and blue flame made Jolene jump back. "Looks like it works." She turned the burner off. "Okay, I'll go to that supermarket over in Couver City. Probably take a couple of hours." Jolene grabbed the keys to the Escalade from the counter. "I don't want to miss the treasure hunt though."

Celeste tore herself away from the letters "Don't worry, It will take us that long to figure this out and find Lily's ghost," she said. "If you're not back, we'll call you and wait for you at the mine."

"Okay, that works." Jolene smiled as she slipped out the door and the rest of them returned to pouring over the letters.

***

Jolene finished loading the groceries in the back of the Escalade and took the cart to the cart corral. Since no one had given her a list, she'd decided on pasta and had loaded her grocery bags with vermicelli, canned sauce, parmesan cheese, garlic bread and cheesecake for desert. She'd also bought some donuts for breakfast the next day.

She didn't buy anything for lunch—maybe she was being overly optimistic about their ability to locate and recover the treasure tonight, but she hoped they'd be packed and on their way back to Maine before noon.

She'd also bought a bag of nacho cheese Doritos, but those were for the ride back to the hotel. Ripping open the bag, she placed it on the console next to her, started the Escalade and pulled out of the grocery store parking lot.

She munched on the tangy chips as she drove down Route 51. The traffic was light and her attention drifted from the road to the desert landscape. The dry, sandy land was a huge contrast to the lush green hills, woods and ocean of her hometown, Noquitt, Maine.

Still, the desert did have some appeal. She liked how the flat contours of the land allowed you to see far into the distance. Like right now, she could see the hill where the mines were even though it was probably more than a mile away.

Jolene crunched off the corner of a Dorito as she looked over at the mines. *Was there a centuries old multi-million dollar treasure there waiting for them?*

A blur of brown caught her eye. She slowed the car, her eyes searching in the direction of the blur. Was that a dog? Scanning the area, she saw it *was* a dog, and it wasn't alone. The two dogs looked just like Emma's dogs, Clive and Lucy. But what would they be doing up at the mine? And where was Emma?

Jolene pulled over to the side of the road and tipped the bag of chips up to her lips, emptying the crumbs into her mouth as she stared over at the hill. It looked like the dogs were running in a frenzied circle around an opening in the hillside opposite the mine entrances she'd explored with her sisters.

After several minutes of staring, she realized Emma was nowhere in sight. Her heart froze as she remembered how Emma said the dogs never went anywhere without her.

Was Emma up there and in trouble?

She shoved the car into drive and peeled out from her spot on the side of the road, the tires squealing as she u-turned to reverse direction and head back toward the road to the mine.

Chapter Fourteen

"Looks like these letters span the six months before Shorty was killed." Celeste pointed to the letters that were now laid out in neat rows on the table.

"It's a true love story." Fiona sighed.

"With a twist," Morgan added. "It looks like the Sheriff was also vying for Lily's attention."

"And making things hard on Shorty." Celeste pointed to a passage in one of the letters. "Here he writes, 'I fear Deke is doing whatever he can to prevent my mining efforts and causing me to be unable to provide for us'."

"Sounds similar to what our favorite Sheriff, Sheriff Kane, is doing right now," Morgan said.

"In this letter, Shorty alludes to Deke trying to run him out of town." Cal pointed to the corner of one of the old letters.

"Wait!" Celeste's heartbeat sped up as she scanned one of the letters they hadn't read yet. "This might be the clue. It talks about the stagecoach robberies."

"What's it say?" Morgan's brow creased as she turned her head sideways to try and read the letter.

"It's written by Lily ... she mentions that she's afraid the robber might come to town." Celeste looked up at the rest of them. "I guess she didn't know the robber was Shorty."

"Was it?" Fiona bent over another of the letters, her read curls cascading over the table. "This letter written by Shorty says he got a tip on when the stage is coming through and he might take a ride out and see if he can confront the robber."

"Maybe he was just saying that so Lily wouldn't be suspicious of him," Cal said.

"Or maybe what Emma said was true and he really wasn't the robber." Morgan frowned down at one of the letters. "Lily says here that, as far as she knows, the sheriff is the only one that knows the stagecoach times in advance."

"This last letter from Lily is kind of ominous," Celeste said. "Lily writes 'we must hasten our plans. Deke said he will stop at *nothing* to make me his ... and our package won't wait'."

Celeste looked at the date of the letter, a heavy rock forming in her chest. "It's dated the day before Deke shot Shorty."

***

Jolene found the road to the other side of the hill easily enough and sped toward where she thought she'd seen the dogs, the Escalade kicking up a cloud of dust in her wake.

She came upon Clive and Lucy running circles outside a dark opening in the hill—a mineshaft they hadn't known about. She jumped out of the car and the dogs ran over to her.

Jolene squatted down to the level of the hounds. "Hey guys, where's Emma?"

Clive licked her hand as she stroked the silky fur on his chest. Lucy whined and looked back over her shoulder at the mine entrance. Jolene could tell the dogs were filled with worry and apprehension.

"Is she in the mine?" Jolene asked the dogs as she squinted into the dark opening. *Of course she was in the mine, where else would she be?*

Jolene stood and walked over to the entrance, the dogs following at her heels.

"Emma?" She yelled into the mine.

The only answer was her own voice echoing hollowly through the tunnels.

She stepped inside. The shaft was wide at the opening, but narrowed pretty quickly. She shuffled in a few feet, noticing the dogs stayed just outside the opening.

"Cowards," she said over her shoulder at them. The dogs whimpered and hung their heads as if they understood.

She forged ahead, calling Emma's name but not getting any response. Where was Emma and why had she come into the mine alone? A shiver danced up her spine as she remembered Emma's insistence that something fishy was going on up here and her vow to investigate.

Maybe she'd fallen and needed help ... or met with foul play. Either way, Jolene had to do her best to help her.

Ten feet in and Jolene couldn't see a thing. She patted her pockets, her heart sinking when she realized she didn't have the little flashlight Luke had given her the other day. She did have one thing though, her Smartphone.

Pulling the phone out of her pocket, she switched it on. The lack of bars told her there was no reception inside the mine, but she didn't want to make a call, she wanted to light the way.

When she'd gotten the phone, Morgan had insisted she install an application that lit up a light on the end of the phone so it could be used like a flashlight. Jolene had thought it was silly, but now she could see how it would come in handy.

"Where is that?" She scrolled through the apps until she found one that looked like a flashlight. She pressed on the icon and a pang of relief shot through her when a bright light came out of the end of the phone. Shining it into the darkness in front of her, she continued on.

It felt like the tunnel walls were closing in on her. It was less than three feet wide and she could reach out and touch both sides. Her heart thudded in her chest as she breathed in the stale, lifeless air. Sweeping the light across the floor and walls, she made slow progress.

"Emma?"

No answer.

Jolene ventured in deeper. She was wondering how far she should go on her own before she backtracked and called for help when the tunnel widened out into some sort of room. Directing the beam of light around in a circle, she could see there were three tunnels off the room.

Which one did Emma take?

She crossed over to the first tunnel and shined the light in. Then repeated it for the next.

Her heart leapt into her throat as she turned to shine her light toward the third tunnel and came face to face with Deputy Styles.

"What are you doing here?" He spoke in a low growly whisper.

Jolene shrank back from him, her stomach sinking.

"What have you done with Emma?" she demanded.

Confusion flickered across his eyes. "Emma? What are you talking about?"

"I know you have her in here." Jolene's eyes darted around the cavern seeking an escape route.

"You shouldn't be in here ... come with me." Styles grabbed her elbow pulling her back toward the way she came.

Jolene jerked her arm away. "Don't touch me!"

Styles stepped back; his hands came up in front of him, palms out. "Whoa there, I'm just trying to make sure you don't get hurt."

His voice was low, barely above a whisper. His eyes darted to the other passages giving him the look of a nervous maniac. She couldn't see his aura, it was too dark in the tunnel but she sensed his energy and she knew he was up to something.

Had Styles discovered Emma in the mine and done something to her? Was he planning to do that same thing to Jolene?

Jolene knew she needed to get away from Styles. She peered over his shoulder anxiously. Her best route of escape was taking the tunnel she'd come in on—at least she knew where that one ended up. But, Styles was standing in front of it blocking her way out.

Jolene did the only other thing she could think of to get away—she pivoted on her heel and ran down one of the tunnels that led further into the mine.

Chapter Fifteen

"What does she mean by 'our package won't wait'?" Morgan asked. "What's in the package?"

"I have no idea." Celeste frowned at the letter. "Maybe it has something to do with the treasure?"

"I still don't see what she wants vindication for," Fiona said.

"I think we need to read between the lines." Cal looked down at the letters. "The letters reveal some things we didn't know, right?"

"Sure, like Lily and Shorty were lovers ... or in love ... or whatever." Morgan made a dismissive gesture with her hand.

"And that Deke wanted Lily for himself," Fiona said.

"So we can conclude that there was friction between Deke and Shorty," Cal added.

"In this letter Lily wrote that Deke would stop at nothing to make her his." Celeste tapped the letter. "So, maybe he didn't shoot Shorty because he was the stagecoach robber, maybe he shot him to get rid of him."

Morgan shot out of her chair. "That's right! She also said that Deke, being Sheriff, was the only one who knew what time the stagecoach was coming.

What if *he* was really the robber and shooting Shorty was just a way of killing two birds with one stone?"

"Playing the hero that killed the robber *and* getting Shorty out of the way so he could have Lily to himself," Fiona said.

"But no more robberies happened after Shorty was killed," Celeste pointed out.

"Even better," Fiona said. "That was a perfect setup. Deke probably already had enough money from the previous robberies, so all he had to do to *prove* he was right about Shorty was to simply not rob any more stagecoaches."

"It's a pretty good plan," Cal added. "No one bothered to look into the robberies any further ... and Deke gets the girl."

"But why *did* he get the girl?" Morgan's brow creased. "From the tone of the letters Lily didn't like Deke much."

Celeste screwed up her face. "That's a good question. And then she remembered seeing the pink stone ring when Lily's ghost put her hand on her stomach ... as if ...

"She was pregnant!" Celeste blurted out. "That was *the package* she referred to in the letter."

"*Shorty's* baby," Fiona said.

"That might explain why she married Deke. She *had* to," Morgan added. "Unwed mothers didn't have a great life back in those days ... and with Shorty dead, she didn't have many options."

"I guess it was lucky for Lily that Deke died two weeks after they married," Fiona said. "At least she got the benefits of being the widow of the Sheriff."

"Was it luck or something else?" Morgan went over to the book about Dead Water and flipped to the section with the pictures. She brought the book over to the table, holding it out. "See this picture of Lily with the garden in the background?"

"Umm hmm."

"Well, look at that plant, right there." Morgan tapped on a section of the photo. "Do you recognize it?"

Celeste pressed her face closer to the book. "That looks like wolfsbane!"

"It *is* wolfsbane," Morgan said. "And we all know what wolfsbane can do."

Celeste nodded. She knew exactly what wolfsbane could do—it was used in herbal remedies, but you had to be very careful because if used in excess it could act as a poison. Morgan had some growing in her herb garden back home and had been falsely accused of using it to kill someone earlier in the year.

"Emma said that Lily was an herbalist ... she knew exactly how to use this plant," Morgan added.

"So, she must have figured out that Deke killed Shorty under false pretenses. Maybe Deke even forced her to marry him somehow. But it looks like she might have gotten back at him in the end." Celeste chuckled.

"I'm kind of glad she did. Deke sounds like a jerk," Fiona added.

"So she wanted vindication for Shorty," Cal said. "To let the world know he wasn't the robber."

"Wait. If Deke was the robber, then does that mean the treasure isn't buried in Shorty's mine?" Fiona looked at them uneasily and Celeste's stomach sank.

What if the treasure wasn't even in the mine and this was all a wild goose chase?

"But then what would the key be for?" Celeste asked.

"Actually, the perfect place for Deke to hide the treasure would be in Shorty's section of the mine. That way he'd be able to come up with extra evidence that Shorty did it, in case anyone else came sniffing around," Cal offered.

"That makes sense," Celeste said. "That explains why Shorty's ghost couldn't see the markings on the wall—Deke must have made them *after* he killed Shorty."

"There's only one way to find out for sure." Cal pushed his chair back and stood. "We need to take a trip to Dead Water and ask Lily."

***

Jolene's heart pounded against her ribcage as she ran down the tunnel, the flashlight illuminating only a couple of feet in front of her. The sounds of Style's voice echoing through the chambers behind her telling her to come back made her run faster.

A split in the tunnel made her stop short.

Left or right?

She bolted into the tunnel on the right and ran smack dab into a wall of hard muscle and flesh.

Jerking back from the arms that tried to grab her, she clenched her hands into fists and brought them up to fight whoever it was. Strong hands clamped on her wrists holding her still.

"Hey now, hold on there."

Jolene gasped as she recognized the voice.

"Kyle? What are *you* doing in here?" Jolene narrowed her eyes at the handsome bartender while relief at seeing a friendly face flooded through her.

Was the whole town in the mine today?

Kyle let go of her wrists and Jolene sucked in a deep breath. She took a step backward, although she had to admit standing that close to Kyle wasn't all that unpleasant. But still, why *was* he here?

"Why were you running? Are you lost?" He answered her question with a question. "And what are *you* doing in here?"

"I saw Emma's dogs outside and thought she might be in here hurt or something," Jolene said. "Have you seen her?"

Kyle's face turned hard at the mention of Emma. "No, but you're right about getting hurt in here. Especially *running* in here. Let me show you the way out."

Kyle grabbed her elbow a little more forcefully than was necessary and Jolene felt a prickle of warning in her gut. She wasn't sure if she should trust him, but he was already pushing her down a small tunnel that led off to the side.

Boots scuffed on the ground behind them and she felt Kyle's hand tense on her elbow.

"You brought the bitch to us ... good work!"

Jolene's blood froze. She spun around to see a dark haired man, his thick mustache hovering over his menacing smile. The large gun in his hand was pointed right at her.

"Bring her this way." The man gestured with his gun to a tunnel on the right. "We'll keep her with the old lady."

Old lady? Did he mean Emma?

Kyle's grip on her elbow grew tighter and she looked up at him with questioning eyes. His face turned hard and he jerked her toward the tunnel.

"Sure, Buck,' Kyle addressed the other man. "I was just trying to get her down there."

What was going on here?

Jolene felt her anger surge. Emma had been right—something *was* going on in the mine and she'd stumbled right into it. God only knew what they'd done to Emma ... and what they had in store for *her*.

With a start, Jolene realized she might have been playing right into Kyle's hands all along. Clearly, these men were here after the treasure. No wonder he had seemed so interested in her—had she given anything away during any of their conversations?

She felt a surge of energy as Kyle shoved her further into the tunnel. Her gift with energy encompassed much more than simply reading people's auras, she could harness energy under certain situations. Like when she was mad or scared. Like now. The problem was, she hadn't learned how to fully control it and she was never sure what would happen once she got into that "state."

Jolene tried to keep her anger in check. She realized that not only were they leading her to Emma, but they might be also taking her straight to the treasure. Better to wait and unleash her angry energy on them when she could keep Emma safe— and after she figured out what they knew about the treasure.

Chapter Sixteen

Celeste's stomach churned with anxiety as Cal drove the Jeep toward Dead Water.

"How are we going to convince Lily to give us the key?" Celeste glanced at Cal, and then turned to look at her sisters in the back seat. "Vindication for Shorty isn't something we can do right away."

"That's a good question," Fiona said. "Did she say what, exactly, she wanted?"

Celeste's brow creased. "No."

"Maybe you need to read between the lines ... like with the letters," Cal offered. "Did she do anything to *show* you what she wanted?"

Celeste pushed back into her seat as she searched her mind for all the interactions she'd had with Lily's ghost. She'd never said anything ... or shown her anything. Wait! Maybe she had ...

"In the cemetery, she was weeping over one of the unmarked graves in the back," Celeste said. "Maybe that was Shorty's grave."

"Probably unmarked because he died a criminal," Morgan added.

"So we could get him a nice headstone," Fiona offered.

"But that's not something we can do this afternoon." Celeste sighed.

"We could correct that book on Dead Water too," Morgan suggested. "You know ... add a new edition or something."

"Maybe, but again, not something we can show Lily right away." Celeste glanced out the window. They were passing Emma's property and she could just see her trailer off in the distance. The sight of it sparked something in her mind. "Well I guess now we know why Shorty left his land to Lily."

Fiona's brows creased together then her face lit. "Of course! He must have had a will made in case something happened ... he knew the sheriff was after him and he wanted to take care of Lily and the baby."

"And that also means that Emma is descended from Shorty ... not the sheriff." Morgan stared out the window as Cal turned onto the road that led to Dead Water.

"She'll probably be happy to hear that," Celeste said. "And to know that her great-grandmother was right to stick by Shorty since he didn't rob the coaches."

"And that she was right all along that the treasure wasn't on her land," Fiona added. "But I wonder how that ring got out there?"

"Good question," Celeste said. As they pulled into Dead Water and parked in the middle of the street, a tingle of nervousness flirted with her stomach.

Would Lily even be here?

She'd never conjured up a ghost before—they usually came to her. Everyone was expecting her to talk to Lily and get the key. She just hoped she wouldn't let them down.

"I'd love to explore all these buildings, but we have more important things to do," Cal said. "How do we get this ghost to come out and show us where the key is?"

Celeste shrugged. "That's a good question. We can start in the saloon. I've seen her there a few times."

They walked over to the old building that was once a thriving saloon. Celeste had been inside so many times she was starting to feel like it was a home away from home. She led the way through the open door and they all stood inside watching the dust motes float in the strips of sunlight.

"Lily?" Celeste ventured. "Are you here?"

Silence.

"We know that Shorty didn't rob the stagecoaches. We can change the book and get him a headstone."

Silence.

"We did our part, now you need to show us the key."

Celeste heard a slight rustling sound, then a thud over by the door. She turned just in time to see a white blur streak past.

"Meow!"

Her breath caught in her throat. "Belladonna!"

She rushed over to the door with her sisters and Cal behind her. They burst out onto the street and looked north. Sure enough, there was Belladonna trotting down the road away from them.

"What is *she* doing here?" Morgan stared at the cat.

"I'm not sure, but I think she might be trying to tell us something." Celeste threw one quick glance over her shoulder into the empty saloon before taking off down the road after the cat.

***

Jolene stumbled into the cavern. Large hands gave a rough push on her back that sent her sprawling to the floor. She glared over her shoulder at Kyle before getting up. Brushing the dirt off her pants, she looked around the room.

This must have been one of the sections of the mine that held larger deposits of gold. It had been chiseled into, drilled out and carved on every section and was large—about twenty feet by twenty feet. Tunnels led off the room in different directions. The cavern itself was lit up with battery-powered lanterns that hung from on the walls. Jolene could see a set of metal tracks that ran into the middle from one of the tunnels. She presumed it was an old system for the carts that would be loaded up with gold and wheeled out.

A cart stood in the middle of the tracks. Loaded. But not with gold.

"Guns? This is about guns?" Jolene looked at the scruffy men who were bent over the cart loading it with various types of weapons. She recognized some as machine guns ... others she had no idea what they were.

Buck laughed, an evil sound that echoed around the cavern. "Yeah. What'd you think it was?"

Jolene noticed everyone staring at her so she just shrugged.

So, keeping them out of the mine wasn't about the treasure after all. The Sheriff didn't want them to discover this gun business ... whatever it was. Surely illegal.

A moan jerked Jolene's attention to the corner and she saw Emma lying in a heap. She rushed over, squatting by the older woman.

"Emma, are you okay?" Jolene pulled her to a sitting position, noticing they'd tied her hands behind her back.

"Yes." Emma nodded. "What are you doing here?"

"I saw Clive and Lucy outside the mine and thought you might be hurt inside," Jolene said.

"Are they okay?" Emma's look of concern for her dogs melted Jolene's heart.

"They're fine," Jolene said. "They wouldn't step a foot inside the mine."

"I guess they're smarter than us, then," Emma said ruefully.

"What is going on in here?" Jolene looked back over her shoulder just in time to see Buck leering at her with a piece of rope in his hand.

"Tie *her* up too." He threw the rope to Kyle. "I'll deal with her after we have these guns loaded up."

Kyle stepped up close to her and spun her around. He grabbed her wrists in a death lock and jerked them back so hard that she cried out, which elicited a laugh from Buck.

"You'll be crying harder than that soon," he said causing the four other men in the room to laugh.

Jolene's stomach curdled. She tried to struggle, but Kyle held her too firmly.

He looped the rope around her wrists, but where she expected to feel the hard bite of them tearing into her flesh, she felt only a light pressure. She looked at Kyle and he shook his head.

He finished with the ropes and pushed her down next to Emma.

"Don't do anything stupid," he whispered than walked away.

Jolene wriggled her wrists—the rope was so loose she could get out of it easily. *Had Kyle tied it loosely on purpose?*

Emma leaned over toward her. "I knew something strange was going on. I saw activity and came up to investigate. Too bad Sheriff Kane found me before I could get a shot off at these guys."

"Kane?" Jolene looked at Emma. "He's behind this?"

"Yep. I guess that's why he didn't want anyone in here and why he wanted to buy up my land and put the hotel out of business," Emma said. "Looks like he's got some black market gun selling business going on out of here and didn't want anyone stumbling on it. I guess my property and the hotel were just too close for comfort."

"Shut up over there!" Buck shouted. He dumped a load of guns onto the cart then thumped his fist on the side and one of the men took off, pushing it out of the cavern.

He sauntered over to Jolene and leaned down in front of her. She gasped as he jerked her up by the arm. Pushing her against the wall he leaned in, his face a fraction of an inch away. His dark, beady eyes drilled into hers and she could smell the stale stench of old food and coffee on his breath.

"I think it might be time to have some fun and show everyone what happens to people who don't mind their own business." His glance moved down to her chest. Jolene's mind whirled a mile a minute despite the churning in her stomach caused by Buck's lustful leer.

She was just about to bring her knee up hard, right where it counts when a large hand slapped itself on Buck's arm, pulling him away.

"Don't lose your head there, buddy." Kyle stared at Buck with hard, cold eyes. "You can have all the fun you want later. Right now we have this shipment to get out."

Chapter Seventeen

Celeste sprinted behind Belladonna. She had a good idea of where the cat was heading but she still didn't want to lose sight of her. At the end of Main Street, the cat turned to the right, headed straight for the graveyard and trotted to the back. She stopped at the grave where they'd seen Lily's ghost days before.

"This is where we came before," Morgan said.

Belladonna blinked at them, waiting for Cal and Fiona, who had fallen behind.

"What's this?" Cal asked as he made his way past the old gravestones.

"We think it's Shorty's grave," Celeste answered. "Lily brought us here the other day."

"Is she here now?" Morgan asked.

Celeste looked around, her mood deflating when she saw no sign of Lily's ghost. "No."

"Lily? Are you here? We figured out how to get vindication for Shorty and now we want you to show us the key." Celeste sighed, crossing her arms across her chest. "We kept our part of the bargain," she added hopefully.

Just then, a wind kicked up a swirl of sand. Belladonna let out a loud "Meow!" and started digging furiously in the sand.

"What the heck?" Celeste squinted at Belladonna. About to pull her away, Celeste saw a wisp of vapor swirling around in front of the cat. *Lily?*

The four of them watched as Belladonna dug about five inches down into the sand, and then hit a granite slab.

"Hey wait a minute," Cal said excitedly. "I think that's the corner of an old grave marker."

He squatted down next to the cat using his hands to scoop away the sand. The girls gathered around, their heads bent as they watched him reveal a fifteen-inch long by six-inch wide slab. Belladonna padded off to the side and started cleaning herself.

"I thought these graves were unmarked back here, but I guess the sand just covered them over after all these years," Morgan said.

"There's no name on it." Celeste frowned down at the granite slab. "It looks like one of those plaques that lay flat on the ground."

Cal started pushing sand away from the front of the marker. The marker was actually two pieces— the top, which was an inch thick slab and then another piece under it that was a little smaller than the top. Cal had revealed two inches of the smaller piece. "No name, but the initials SH are right here on the front."

"Shorty Hanson!" Fiona exclaimed.

"Yeah, but how does this get us closer to the key?" Morgan asked.

The four of them stared at each other for a few seconds ... or five of them counting Belladonna. Finally, the cat strolled over to the marker and lay down across it, her paw dangling over one corner.

"Mew."

Celeste saw Cal's eyes go wide as he watched the cat.

"That's it!" He reached over to where Belladonna's paw dangled and grabbed the corner underneath the slab. Wiggling his hand back and forth, he grunted and bent down almost level with the ground, then pushed and shoved.

Celeste gasped as she heard the scrape of granite on granite and saw Cal pull out a piece of the marker to reveal a small compartment, like a drawer. Inside was an old rolled up piece of paper and a small book.

"Wow, look at that." Morgan reached into the drawer and pulled the two items out.

Cal straightened up, brushing the sand from his hands. "Putting special drawers in gravestones is an old and not often used custom. I would never have guessed a gravestone in the old west would have one, but when I saw Belladonna practically pointing to this section of the stone I figured I should look."

Celeste smiled. She'd known Cal's expertise as a history buff would come in handy.

"Why would someone want to put a drawer in a gravestone?" Fiona asked.

Cal laughed. "Well normally, it's for loved ones to put mementos in ... stuff they don't want to just leave out in the elements on top of the grave. But in this case, it looks like it was used for something else entirely."

"I'll say." Morgan carefully unrolled the piece of paper and angled it toward Cal. "Does this look like the key you need to decrypt those symbols in the mine?"

Cal stared at the paper, the corners of his lips curling up in a smile. "Ladies, I think we've found the key."

"So I guess Lily came through with her end of the bargain." Celeste slid her eyes over to Belladonna. "Although in kind of a roundabout way."

"I guess so." Cal pushed the little drawer back into place and replaced the sand he'd moved around. "Now let's get over to the mine and see if we can use this key to figure out where the treasure is."

***

Kyle shoved Jolene back to the ground beside Emma and shot her a look of warning before he walked off.

What was that about?

Jolene glanced over at Emma who appeared to be working at the ropes behind her back.

"What are you doing?" she whispered.

"I found a rough chipped rock and I'm rubbing the ropes. We gotta get away."

"Hold on," Jolene said. "I'm almost out of mine, but we need to time things carefully. Wait until I give the signal."

Jolene kept her eye on Buck, Kyle and the others while she wriggled her hands out of the rope. Cartons of guns, ammunition and, Jolene assumed, other weapons were stacked up on one side of the cave. It looked like they were loading them onto the carts to move them out ... to where?

Jolene guessed there was a truck waiting at the other end of the tunnel. Kane must be using the empty mines as a storage place for guns he was clearly selling illegally.

Jolene's stomach clenched as she looked around. There were six men including Kyle and Buck and they were all armed.

Could she and Emma win against six of them?

"Hurry up," Buck snapped. "We need to get this shipment out in the next hour."

"Then next week do it all over again," one of the men said.

"That's what pays the bills." Buck grunted as he hefted a heavy crate onto his shoulder and walked it to the cart.

What would happen once they were done moving the guns? They'd turn their attention to her and Emma. Jolene knew she would have to make her move before then, but what, exactly was she going to do?

She noticed Kyle giving her looks out of the corner of his eye and prayed he didn't suspect that she'd wriggled free.

Jolene closed her eyes and summoned all her energy. She knew that if she thrust out her hands, an arc of energy would burst out jolting anything in its wake. The problem was she didn't have much control over where the energy went and inside the mine with all the ammunition that could be dangerous. She didn't want to blow up the whole mine, especially with her and Emma in there.

A movement inside one of the tunnels caught her eye and she turned to see Deputy Styles hovering just inside the tunnel. Jolene's heart lurched—once he joined them, she'd be outnumbered seven to one. She looked back at the men.

They were almost done loading the crates into the cart, she couldn't wait until they moved the cart out—it was now or never.

***

Celeste, Cal, Morgan, Fiona and Belladonna sprinted to the Jeep.

Fiona pulled out her cell phone. "I'll call the others and let them know to meet us at the mine."

Cal's phone chirped as he whipped the car onto the road. He picked it up, looking at the display.

"Looks like I've got a message ... maybe it's from Luke." He pressed the button and stuck the phone to his ear.

Celeste glanced over in time to see him frown. "Is something wrong?"

He put the phone away and shook his head. "Not really. That was my attorney and she said she couldn't find anything about the rezoning of the hotel."

"Darn it! Jolene's not answering," Fiona said from the back. "I'll send her a text. Luke and Jake are going to meet us there."

"Hey what was that book you found?" Celeste turned to face Morgan who was leafing through the small book with Belladonna sleeping on her lap.

"It's a diary ... Lily's diary," Morgan said without looking up from the book.

"Really? Does it say why she married the sheriff ... and if she had Shorty's baby?" Celeste asked.

"I don't know." Morgan flipped a page. "I haven't gotten to that part yet. It starts when she comes to Dead Water. She was an accomplished singer, you know. Came to sing in the saloon."

Celeste's heart tugged as she pictured a young, innocent Lily coming out west to sing, then meeting Shorty and falling in love ... until Deke ruined it. She turned back around to face forward. They were almost at the mine and soon they'd have the treasure for Luke's company. *Then* they could work on getting the vindication that Lily wanted.

She felt her heart rate bump up with the excitement of finding hidden treasure. It wasn't about the money—she had plenty of that already—it was about the thrill of the chase. Oh sure, they'd be paid well for the job, but Celeste liked the excitement more than the paycheck. She had no idea what Luke's company would do with it after they found it, but she'd been told they usually restored most of the treasure to the rightful owners —after taking a generous finder's fee, of course. She liked the thought of that ... maybe some of it would even go to Lily's heirs.

Cal pulled the Jeep to a stop, interrupting her thoughts and everyone jumped out and ran for the mineshaft that Celeste had found the symbols in.

Then they stopped short.

"No one else is here ... should we wait?" Morgan peered into the mine.

Fiona shaded her eyes and looked down the road. "I don't even see any dust. It might be a while."

Cal had the paper with the key to the symbols already unrolled in his hand.

"I don't see the harm in going in and doing some preliminary scouting," he said. "We'll be that much further ahead when they get here."

The four of them ran into the mine. No one noticed Belladonna following silently behind them —they were too intent on the symbols on the wall.

Celeste aimed the beam of her flashlight on the symbols on the wall and Fiona shone hers on the paper Cal held. Cal looked back and forth between the wall and the paper.

"Okay, I think I've got it," he said. "This middle symbol is like an arrow ... it tells you the direction. But the first symbol coincides with a letter. I think A is for the first marking, B for the second etc. The last symbol I believe is like a yes or no. Yes means we should follow the direction of the arrow ... no means we should not."

Celeste made a face. She didn't really understand any of it. "Okay, if you say so."

"So, if I'm right, we should take this tunnel here." Cal pointed to the tunnel on the right, and then looked at the sisters.

"Sounds good to me." Morgan shrugged and headed off to the right.

They repeated the process at the next fork with Cal interpreting the symbols from the key and then directing them down one of the tunnels.

As Celeste followed Cal's instructions through the maze of tunnels, she felt a seed of doubt take root in her stomach. She trusted Cal and knew he was an expert with codes ... but what if he was wrong this time?

They hadn't made any marks so that they could find their way back, and if Cal's interpretation of the key was incorrect, they could be lost in the mine forever.

***

Jolene let the rope fall from her wrists. She shot her hands out in front of her and yelled. "Stop!"

An arc of energy shot out toward Buck like a bolt of hot, white lightening. It struck him in the chest, knocking him off balance. Kyle's eyes widened as he watched Buck fall. He turned toward Jolene and she saw the startled look of surprise in his eyes as he reached for his gun.

Jolene heard the click of pistols and her heart stalled in her chest when she noticed all four of the men were aiming their guns at her.

"Take this!" Emma yelled from beside Jolene as she hurled a large rock at one of the men, striking him in the head and knocking him to his knees.

Jolene put her hands up, ready to aim them at the first man who approached. Out of the corner of her eye, she saw Styles run into the cavern, his gun out. But something was strange ... instead of pointing the gun at her as she expected, he was pointing it at the gun runners—and so was Kyle.

The gun runners must not have noticed, though, because the three left standing were advancing on Jolene. She squeezed her eyes shut and thrust out her hands to ward them off.

She heard Kyle say, "Get back and put your hands up—the party's over."

And then the cavern exploded with a deafening boom.

Chapter Eighteen

As Celeste followed Cal down another tunnel, her earlier doubts took root and she decided to voice her concern that they should turn back and wait for the others, or at least come up with some sort of plan to backtrack their way out.

"Hey, you guys, I think we should—"

Kaboom!

Celeste's heart leapt into her throat. "What was that?"

"It sounded like some sort of an explosion and I think it came from straight ahead!" Cal sprinted in the direction of the noise "Come on!"

Celeste took off after him following him down the tunnel, around a turn and out into a large cavern. Her heart stopped when she looked across the cavern and saw—

"Jolene!" Celeste stared at her sister who was standing about fifteen feet away, her hands up to her ears and her eyes screwed shut. Jolene opened one eye tentatively, then the other, both eyes growing wide when she spotted Celeste.

"What are *you* doing here?" Jolene asked.

"We were following the markings in the tunnel." Celeste surveyed the room. Five men lay on the floor. Two were on their stomachs, hands cuffed behind their backs. Two others were being handcuffed—she recognized one of the men doing the handcuffing as Deputy Styles. The fifth lay on his back out cold with an ugly welt forming on his forehead.

"What the heck is going on here?" Morgan demanded, as she walked over to the cart full of guns.

"We caught a bunch of gun runners, that's what's going on." Emma stood from where she had been crouching next to Jolene and brushed dust off her pants, holding out the side of her shirt that had a big hole in it. "And someone shot at us."

"What?" Fiona narrowed her eyes at Jolene and Emma. "How did you guys get in here and *why* are you hanging around with gun runners?"

Celeste saw Jolene glance nervously at the two men who were doing the handcuffing.

"Wait ... you guys are both *good* guys?" Jolene asked, narrowing her eyes in disbelief.

"That's right." The one who Celeste didn't recognize jerked the cuffs tightly on his captive and stood up. "I'm Kyle Donahue ... FBI."

Jolene gasped. "Wait a minute ... you're not in the FBI, you're the bartender."

Kyle favored her with a lopsided smile and spread his hands at his sides. "Just a cover."

"B-but you dragged me in here and tied me up." Jolene sputtered.

"Yeah, sorry about that. I was trying to get you out of the mine when Buck caught us." Kyle grimaced. "I had no choice but to bring you here or it would have blown my cover. But, I did try to keep the ropes loose."

"What about Emma?" Jolene's forehead creased as she put her arm around the older woman.

"Oh that ugly one, Buck, found me in the mine. I'd seen the strange activity and decided to investigate. He wasn't so nice with the ropes." Emma rubbed her wrists and Celeste's heart tugged when she saw the raw red marks the rope had left.

"And what about you?" Jolene turned to Deputy Styles. "You tried to grab me in the tunnel!"

"Yes, I was trying to get you out of here so you wouldn't get hurt with all this going on." He waved his hands around to indicate the guns. "But you bolted."

"So, *this* is why you threatened to arrest us if we went into the mine?" Celeste asked Styles.

Styles nodded. "Yep. I've been working with the FBI for months to blow the lid off this operation ...

I couldn't risk you guys coming in and messing it up or getting yourselves hurt."

"And Sheriff Kane was working with the FBI too?" Fiona asked.

"Oh no." Kyle shook his head. "He's the ringleader of this operation. My main goal was to catch him."

Celeste stared at the men on the floor. Kane wasn't among them. "But he's not here."

"That's right ... we were waiting for Kane to get here so we'd have the proof to arrest him, but someone ..." Kyle slid his eyes over to Jolene. "Took it upon themselves to stir things up and we had to move forward with our plan prematurely. He's probably already gotten word about what happened and hightailed it out of town."

"And that's why Kane wanted me to move off my land and why he wanted to close down the hotel," Emma said. "So no one would see the comings and goings of his gun operation."

"It was in his best interest to make sure no one noticed what was going on here," Kyle said, his eyes narrowing at Celeste. "I know Emma came here because she saw activity and wanted to investigate, and Jolene saw Emma's dogs and came in thinking Emma might need help ... but what are the rest of you doing here?"

Celeste exchanged an uneasy glance with her sisters and Cal. Morgan and Fiona shrugged.

"We might as well tell them ... it's not like it's a secret,' Cal said. "We were following some markings in the mine shafts that we hoped would lead us to a buried treasure."

"Buried treasure?" Deputy Styles laughed. "I doubt there's anything like that down here. Otherwise someone would have found it by now."

Kyle glanced at Jolene. "I figured all that talk in the bar about you and your sisters being history buffs was a ruse. You're much too pretty to be a geeky history buff. But an adventurous treasure hunter? That suits you much better."

Celeste's lips tugged into a smile as she watched Jolene's cheeks turn a touch of pink. There wasn't much that could make her sister blush.

"Well, it's not like I was lying ... I just didn't know how much I should say. And I do like history," Jolene said. "But it's really Luke that—"

Jolene stopped in mid-sentence a puzzled look on her face. "Hey, where *is* Luke ... and Jake?"

"Oh shoot!" Morgan said. "We were supposed to meet them at the mine entrance. I better go get them!"

"Wait!" Cal yelled as she hurried into the tunnel. "We'll have to use the symbols to lead us back. I'll go with you."

"Symbols?" Kyle asked as Cal and Morgan disappeared into the tunnel.

Celeste explained about the symbols on the tunnel walls and how they'd found the key to decode them in Dead Water to Kyle. She left out the part about the ghosts.

"Thanks to those letters, we figured out what really happened with the robberies back in 1878," Celeste said to Emma. "You were right about Shorty not being the robber."

"Ha! I *knew* it!" Emma beamed. "But who *was* the robber, then?"

"We're pretty sure it was the Sheriff, Deke," Fiona said.

Emma laughed. "Seems like this area has a propensity for crooked sheriffs."

"Speaking of which," Kyle said as he hauled one of the gun runners up onto his feet. "Styles and I better take these guys out and get them processed. I'll need you all to stick around town for a few days so I can get some statements."

Everyone murmured their consent as Kyle and Styles hauled the bad guys and the cart full of guns off in the direction of the tracks. Just before he disappeared into the dark tunnel, Kyle turned around. "I hope to see you again, Jolene."

Did *she* want to see *him* again? Jolene squinted at him, trying to see his aura. Still yellow. Jolene doubted she'd want to take up with the handsome FBI agent, but she shot him a half smile just in case she changed her mind.

As Kyle disappeared down one tunnel, Cal and Morgan appeared in the other leading Luke, Jake, Buzz and Gordy all armed with metal detectors and shovels.

"Cal tells me you guys had an exciting afternoon," Luke said.

Jolene shrugged. "All in a day's work."

Luke chuckled. "Well, no one said anything about busting up a ring of gun runners when they told me about this job but I guess you gotta do what you gotta do."

"So just where is this treasure?" Jake slipped over to Fiona's side and slid his arm around her shoulders.

Cal peeked back out into the tunnel, looked at the walls, and then double-checked the paper in his hand. "If this key is correct, the treasure is right here in this room."

"Well if that don't beat all," Emma said. "Sheriff Kane was going to all this trouble to sell guns illegally—chasing away anyone who came to the mine and trying to get me to sell out, when the whole time he was sitting on a treasure cache."

"That *is* ironic." Celeste looked around the large cavern. "But if it's in here … where would it be?"

Buzz hefted his metal detector. "That's why we have these."

"Meow."

Celeste whipped around in the direction of the sound. "How did Belladonna get in here?"

"She must have hopped out of the car and followed us down the tunnel," Morgan said.

"I think she might be trying to tell us something," Fiona added as the cat sprinted over to a corner and started scratching in the hard dirt floor.

Celeste narrowed her eyes. Just behind Belladonna a white swirly mist appeared. A ghost? No, too wide to be a ghost. Wait! It was two ghosts. As the apparitions took form, Celeste recognized them as Lily and Shorty. Together.

The ghosts looked straight at her and smiled. Shorty took Lily's hand and Lily mouthed the words "Thank you", and then pointed down to where Belladonna was digging just as they started to disappear.

"That's where the treasure is!" Celeste rushed over to Belladonna. Gordy, Buzz, Jake and Luke followed with their metal detectors. Luke's detector emitted a series of beeps as he ran it over the area.

"There's something here," he said. He swung the detector in a wide arc, then again, using a smaller arc, then an even smaller one, letting the detector's beeps help him pinpoint where to dig.

"Here." He scratched an x in the compacted dirt floor with his boot and Buzz and Gordy descended on it with shovels.

The floor was hard and the digging went slowly. Celeste and the others hovered around behind Buzz and Gordy. Belladonna curled up next to one of the tunnels and went to sleep.

Celeste was starting to wonder if the ghosts had played a trick on her when she heard the hollow thud of metal on wood.

"I think I've got something!" Buzz put down his shovel and knelt beside the hole. Luke joined him, brushing dirt aside to reveal the corner of a wooden trunk.

"It's a trunk of some sort." Luke looked up at them excitedly. "The treasure could be inside."

They continued digging, this time more carefully, around the edges of the trunk. Made out of oak, the trunk was edged in brass and had wide brass bands around the middle. It was about four feet long and two feet wide—too heavy for the men to lift out from above.

Celeste's stomach pinged with impatient anticipation as they dug a trench along either side of the trunk. Finally, Gordy and Luke jumped into the trench and lifted the box out, its shiny brass hinges on the back facing into the cavern.

"Dang, this thing is heavy," Gordy said.

"If this thing is full of gold it's gonna be worth a fortune." Luke tilted his head, assessing the side of the box. He curled his fingers under the lid to open it but the lid wouldn't budge.

"Give me a hand here." Luke motioned for Buzz to lift on the other side of the lid. "I think this thing is stuck."

Celeste walked around to the side of the trunk and craned her neck to see the front, which was sitting about six inches away from the wall. A large, square brass escutcheon with a fleur-de-lis design sat below the lid—a huge keyhole in the middle indicated they would need a skeleton key to open the box.

"I think it's locked." Celeste pointed to the front of the trunk and Luke and Gordy leaned over to look.

"I guess so." Luke pushed the box around so the keyhole was facing them.

"Pfft. That's easy. A child could break into that kind of lock." Jolene approached the box. "Just give me something long and pointy and I'll have it open in no time."

"Wait a minute." Emma pulled out a long chain she'd been wearing around her neck. On the end dangled a large skeleton key ... with the same fleur-de-lis design as the escutcheon on the box. "Maybe this will work."

Jolene took the key from Emma. "It matches the box."

"It was my great-grandma's ... Lily. She gave it to my grandmother who passed it along to me." Emma shrugged. "She told me Lily always said it was important, but I never dreamed it might open a treasure."

Jolene inserted the key into the lock. *Click.* Jolene turned the key and lifted the top. Celeste sucked in a breath as she looked inside ... it was loaded with pebbles of gold, silver and a few pieces of jewelry. She recognized the Vanderbeek necklace in the pile.

Celeste felt happiness bubble up into her throat ... until she heard the unmistakable sound of a gun being cocked behind her.

"Hold it right there!"

Chapter Nineteen

Celeste whipped around, her heart sinking when she saw Dixie Sumner standing just outside one of the tunnel entrances pointing a gun at them.

"Dixie!" Morgan gasped.

"What are you doing?" Celeste's brows furrowed together. Had Dixie come to catch the gun runners? If so, why was she holding her gun on *them*?

"I came to claim what's rightfully mine." Dixie glared at them.

"Rightfully yours?" Fiona cast a perplexed look around the room.

"That's right." Dixie thrust her chin in the direction of the treasure. "Great-Grandma was a Vanderbeek before she married Matthias Brandt. That chest has her jewelry plus gold and silver my family had on those coaches."

Dixie thrust the gun out toward them and Celeste noticed scratches on her wrist—just like a cat's claw would make.

"You're the one who broke into our room at the hotel!" Celeste pointed to the scratches. "Belladonna must have scratched you." Celeste glanced over at the cat who was sitting on her haunches eyeing Dixie through angry, half-slitted eyes.

"What?" Morgan craned to see Dixie's wrist. "Why would you break into our room in your own hotel?"

"I knew what you guys were up to right from the start." Dixie spit out the words. "Trying to come here and steal the treasure. I figured I could find the answers on your computers and notes ... but I had to make it look like a regular break-in. Lucky thing my message didn't scare you guys off because I didn't get everything I needed from your computer. That's when I decided to try to help you out with the book on Dead Water. I figured I'd give you folks what you needed and let you do all the work. It's a good thing you people are so persistent ... All's I had to do was wait patiently and you led me right to the treasure."

Celeste's stomach churned at the smug look on Dixie's face. How could they have been so stupid? She'd even wanted to invest some money in the hotel to help her.

"Oh, and thanks for the new couch and chairs too. Saved me from having to spend any of this treasure money to buy them myself. Now, if you'll step away from my treasure ..." Dixie gestured wildly with her gun.

Celeste's heart raced as she glanced at the others. They couldn't let Dixie get away with the treasure after all this work, but none of them had a weapon ... except Jolene. Glancing sideways at her sister, she saw Jolene push her hands out. Celeste knew what could happen when Jolene was mad— the energy could be powerful. She braced herself, staring at Jolene's hands and waiting.

Nothing happened.

Jolene frowned at her hands and pushed them out in front of her again.

Nothing.

Celeste's stomach sank. How could they get the gun away from Dixie?

Something behind Dixie caught Celeste's eye. A shadow ... was it a ghost? Then she heard a click and a familiar deep male voice said. "Put the gun down, Dixie."

Celeste saw Dixie's face redden with anger as she whirled around, revealing the person who was standing behind her.

"Mateo?" Celeste stared down into the tunnel incredulously. Mateo had come to their aid before ... always seeming to show up just at the right time. But how had he even known they were here?

Dixie faced Mateo in anger, but kept her gun trained on them ... Jolene in particular.

"Back off or the brunette gets it." Dixie divided her attention between Mateo and Jolene.

"Come on Dixie, you don't want to do that. You'd be dead before the bullet even leaves your gun." Mateo's gun never wavered as he kept it trained on Dixie.

Celeste could see the uncertainty on Dixie's face as her eyes darted from Mateo to Jolene. The gun started to waver and then Celeste heard a low growl from behind Dixie. Celeste's heart leaped into her throat when she saw Belladonna hurl herself toward Dixie's gun.

"Belladonna! No!" Celeste heard Morgan scream ... and then Dixie fired the gun.

***

The sound of the gunshot hit Celeste like a punch in the gut. Tears pricked her eyes as she stared in Dixie's direction, expecting to see Belladonna crumpled in a bloody heap on the floor. But instead, the cat was clinging onto Dixie's arm while the hapless hotel owner tried to shake her off.

Dixie dropped her gun in the scuffle and Jake leapt forward, picking it off the ground and training it on its owner.

Mateo took the opportunity to grab Dixie from behind and shove her free arm up behind her.

"I knew I never should have rented you a room!" Dixie spat in his face as she struggled to get free.

"Meow." Belladonna dropped from Dixie's arm, landing softly on her feet and padding over to sit in front of the treasure chest. Celeste bent down and scooped her up, kissing the top of her head.

"You're the other guest at the hotel?" Morgan raised her brows at Mateo.

Mateo shot her a smile. "Someone has to keep you girls out of trouble."

"Hey, wait a minute." Jolene narrowed her eyes at Mateo. "Have you been following us?"

Mateo pressed his lips together as he pulled handcuffs out of his back pocket and cuffed Dixie's hands behind her back. "I wouldn't exactly call it *following*. Our paths are destined to cross. You'll see."

He nodded at Jake before shoving Dixie in his direction. "I trust that you can get our friend here to the proper authorities."

Then Mateo nodded at Celeste and her sisters, turned and disappeared into the dark tunnel.

"Hey, wait!" Jolene sprinted after him.

Emma watched Jolene. "Well you people are a lot of fun, and this treasure sure is pretty, but the real treasure in my life is my dogs, so I suppose I should get out of here and make sure they're okay. I wonder if they're still waiting for me outside the mine."

Jolene came sprinting back into the cavern. "He got away. I've never seen anyone disappear as fast as that guy. What's with him, anyway?"

Celeste shrugged. "Who knows … he sure does seem to disappear pretty quickly but I'm glad he showed up when he did."

Jolene screwed her face up. "Yeah, but I wonder what he meant about our path's being destined to cross."

"Some things are better found out in due time," Emma said to Jolene. "I gotta go check on my dogs, but I want to thank you for risking your life to come in here and help me."

"Aww … It was no problem." Jolene and Emma hugged.

"Can you find your way out?" Celeste asked.

"Oh, sure," Emma said releasing Jolene and heading toward one of the tunnels, "I know my way around here pretty good. See you folks later."

Emma stopped in front of Dixie on her way out and fixed her with a glare. "You know, I knew you were no good … just like your Momma. Papa said you and she influenced my grandma to disown him so you could have all the family money and I never wanted to believe it. But I guess he was right." Then she disappeared down one of the tunnels.

"We'll come by to drop those letters off tomorrow," Morgan shouted after her.

"Well I better find someplace where there's cell phone service so I can call the home office and tell them we found the treasure." Luke looked at Buzz and Gordy. "Can you guys stand guard until we figure out how to catalogue it and pack it up?"

"Sure boss," Buzz said.

"And I better get Dixie to the sheriff," Jake added.

"And we better get Belladonna back to the hotel so we can give her a big treat for being so brave," Morgan added, taking the cat from Celeste.

Cal slipped his arm around Celeste as they all started out of the tunnel.

"Boy there sure were a lot of buried secrets around here,' Celeste said.

"Yeah." Cal squeezed her close. "This was fun, but I can't wait to get back home and have everything back to normal."

"Me too," Celeste said "But there's one thing I have to do first."

"What's that?"

"I have to keep my promise to a ghost." Celeste looked over her shoulder into the cavern. The misty figures of Lily and Shorty stood next to the treasure watching her. She winked at them and then they turned around, and walked away arm in arm, their figures fading slowly until they finally disappeared.

Epilogue

Jolene wiped the sweat from her forehead as she watched the intricately carved headstone with Shorty's name, birth and death dates being lowered into place. Glancing back toward the deserted town of Dead Water, she watched as a tumbleweed rolled across the street.

It was silent except for the sounds of the machinery and the discontented mewls coming from Belladonna who sat unhappily trapped in her cat carrier at Jolene's feet. Jolene could hardly blame the cat, but they were on their way to the airport after this and they'd had to secure her in the crate. Buzz and Gordy had already gone ahead with the luggage—all she had to do was get the cat there safely and she couldn't risk her wandering off. As Jolene breathed in a lungful of the dry, stifling desert air, she felt a pinch of longing for home. She could hardly wait to get out of here.

"I hope this gives Lily ... and Shorty, some peace," Celeste said as she helped settle the stone into the hole where the old marker had been.

"It's a beautiful stone." Fiona ran her fingers across the marble carving on the top. "I don't know what more we could do."

"Except hopefully get another edition of the Dead Water book written," Morgan added.

"Hopefully that will satisfy them and they won't come back to haunt us," Jolene joked.

Celeste laughed. "Well I think Lily and Shorty are all set ... Deke, on the other hand might not be too happy."

"Yeah, he wasn't a nice ghost," Fiona said. "But in the long run he actually helped us figure out where the treasure was and helped get Shorty's name cleared."

"How do you figure that?" Jolene's forehead pleated as she looked at her sister.

"Well, he was the one that told Celeste to look near Shorty's homestead. If he hadn't done that, we would have never found the pink ring or met Emma. And if *that* never happened, we might never have gotten Emma to trust us with the letters."

Jolene nodded. "True, I guess he did help our cause."

"Seems like he and Sheriff Kane would have gotten along just fine," Cal said. "Did they ever find Kane?"

Emma shook her head. "Nope. Just like that FBI guy said, he must have gotten wind of what was going on and high-tailed it out of here."

"That explains why Buzz and Gordy saw him loading his car with boxes and head out on the highway when I had them tailing him," Luke said. "Too bad I didn't know what he was really up to or I could have had them stop him."

"What was he doing with all those guns, anyway?" Fiona asked.

Luke shrugged. "Turns out he was selling them to militant groups ... illegally of course. He was using his connections in law enforcement to get used guns cheap and selling them to the groups for a profit. It can be quite lucrative."

"No doubt," Cal said. "And he had the perfect place to store them—in the old gold mines."

"Yep, the railway carts were still there and he could stockpile the guns inside the mine and then when he made a sale, he used the carts to move them out to trucks waiting at the entrance of the mine," Luke added.

"So, was Dixie really making up all the stuff about Kane trying to close the hotel?" Morgan asked.

"Well, not everything," Jake said. "When I finally handed her over to Deputy—I mean *Sheriff* —Styles I found out that Kane really was trying to drive her out. Just as we suspected, he didn't want people anywhere near the mines and, even though the hotel was far away, it was on the one road that led to them. Guess he figured his operation would be safer if no one was on that road to see his comings and goings."

"But she did make up the part about the rezoning meeting," Luke added. "She used that as an alibi. Of course if we'd double-checked that we might have suspected she was up to something sooner."

"But she seemed so nice," Celeste said. "I felt sorry for her ... we even wanted to invest some money in the hotel!"

"Unfortunately her mamma had a big influence on her." Emma's face hardened and her eyes got a faraway look. "Dixie's mother was my second cousin ... or something like that. Anyway, she was an angry, bitter person and for some reason she hated my father. I never got the real story, but somehow she got my grandparents to turn against my father."

Jolene's heart tugged at the sad look on Emma's face.

"She carried a lot of bitterness and hatred her whole life. I guess it just ate away at her and she ended up going over the edge. She was obsessed with getting back what she thought was rightfully hers" Emma said. "I guess she meant the necklace and whatever else was stolen in the robberies."

"Ironically, she would have gotten it anyway," Luke answered. "My employers return any treasure recovered to the rightful owners provided they have indisputable evidence."

Jolene narrowed her eyes at Luke. "Well, if that's the case, won't the necklace go to Emma, now? Or at least to the other descendants of the Vanderbeek woman?"

Luke smiled. "Yes it will. In fact, I've already looked into it and it appears Emma is the only direct descendant left. I've talked to my boss and he's arranging it so you get the necklace."

Jolene felt her heart swell as she looked at Emma. "Emma, that necklace is worth millions!"

Emma smiled. "Well I can't say I have much use for *millions*—I'll probably donate most of it to the local animal shelter. Money don't mean much to me. I'm more grateful that you girls found out the truth about my family and found this." Emma held up the little diary they'd found hidden in the old grave marker.

"There's one thing that bugs me," Morgan said. "Why didn't Lily ever look for the treasure?"

Emma tapped the diary on her hand. "In here it says she hated that treasure for everything it caused her. She didn't want to have anything to do with it."

"Did she say Deke forced her to marry him?" Fiona asked.

"In a way," Emma replied. "She really felt she had no other choice. Deke had promised to make life miserable for her if she refused. And she was pregnant. Of course, she didn't let Deke know about *that*. She suspected he was the robber all along, but after she married him she found out he was for sure."

"So she took the key and handed it down to her granddaughter." Fiona said it more as a statement than a question.

"Yes. And she made sure Deke would never enjoy the treasure," Emma said grimly.

"With the wolfsbane she grew in her garden?" Morgan raised a brow at Emma.

Emma nodded. "She did what she had to do."

"Well everything seems to be much clearer now." Celeste pursed her lips. "Except the part about Mateo being a guest at the hotel and showing up in the mine."

"I guess he was the one asking about us in the bar," Jolene said. "Unless that was another thing that Kyle made up. But I still think it's strange that he'd be at the hotel and not let us know. I mean why all the mystery?"

"Yeah, and he sure cleared out of there fast," Fiona said. "I would have liked to have thanked him for his help, but he was gone before we got back ... almost like he was never there in the first place ... like some sort of ghost."

"He sure is mysterious," Morgan added. "But don't worry, I have a feeling we'll be seeing him again."

"Well, now that I've read the diary, I think it really belongs back in here." Emma squatted down beside the headstone, now firmly set in place, and pulled open a hidden drawer, just like the one in the original marker. She slid the diary in, then slipped the key from the chain on her neck and added that. Cal bent down and added the paper that held the key to decoding the symbols.

"Well, I guess that's it, then." Celeste patted the top of the headstone and turned to walk away. "Rest in peace, Shorty. Our job here is done."

Jolene picked up Belladonna's carrier eliciting an angry meow from the cat and followed them to the cars that were parked several feet away at the edge of the cemetery.

They bid Emma good-bye and Jolene loaded Belladonna into the Escalade, and then piled in with her sisters while the Luke and Jake took the Jeep.

Jolene settled into the back seat as Fiona, who had wrestled the keys from Morgan on the way out of the hotel, drove away from the ghost town.

"Well this was certainly an interesting trip." Morgan twisted in the passenger seat to face Jolene and Celeste in the back.

"That's for sure," Celeste answered.

Jolene saw Morgan's eyes narrow as they drifted to her throat and her hands flew up there instinctively. She felt the cold metal of the necklace she was wearing—a silver heart shaped locket with a garnet stone.

"Where did you get that?" Morgan's brows creased in a V as she reached out to touch the locket.

"I found Belladonna batting it around in the room when I was packing this morning," Jolene said, a strange feeling taking root in her stomach as she leaned forward in her seat to let Morgan inspect the locket. "It must have been in the suitcase, I guess."

Jolene saw a shadow passed over Morgan's eyes. "That's just like the one Mom always wore."

"It is?" Jolene frowned down at the locket. She'd been a self-absorbed teenager when her mother died and hadn't noticed the jewelry she wore. Well, not consciously anyway, but that explained why the locket had seemed so familiar when she first saw it.

Celeste leaned forward to look at the necklace and Jolene heard her sharp intake of breath. She saw Fiona angle the rear-view mirror so that she could get a look at it too. "It is!" both sisters said at once.

"But that's impossible." Morgan's voice trembled. "She was wearing it when ..."

Morgan's voice trailed off and Jolene's stomach twisted. Her mother had jumped to her death from the cliffs outside their seaside home, and if she'd been wearing this necklace ... well, it would have been smashed on the rocks or lying at the bottom of the ocean.

"Well, there are probably plenty of lockets that look like it. I'm sure it's just a coincidence," Fiona said.

"Right, of course." The relief was evident in Morgan's eyes.

"Yeah, it couldn't be the same locket ... that would just be too weird," Celeste said.

Right. It was just a strange coincidence, Jolene thought as she sank back into her seat and tried to squelch the nervousness that lapped at her stomach.

As she stared out at the passing desert scenery, she tried to convince herself there was no reason to get nervous over a crazy coincidence.

And she might have succeeded too, except there was just one problem ... she didn't believe in coincidences.

The end.

**

Want more Blackmoore Sister's adventures? Buy the rest of the books in the series:

Dead Wrong (Book 1)
Dead & Buried (Book 2)
Dead Tide (Book 3)

Sign up for my newsletter and find out how to get my latest releases at the lowest discount price:

http://www.leighanndobbs.com/newsletter

About The Author

Leighann Dobbs discovered her passion for writing after a twenty year career as a software engineer. She lives in New Hampshire with her husband Bruce, their trusty Chihuahua mix Mojo and beautiful rescue cat, Kitty. When she's not reading, gardening or selling antiques, she likes to write romance and cozy mystery novels and novelettes which are perfect for the busy person on the go.

Find out about her latest books and how to get discounts on them by signing up at:

http://www.leighanndobbs.com/newsletter

Connect with Leighann on Facebook and Twitter

http://facebook.com/leighanndobbsbooks

http://twitter.com/leighanndobbs

More Books By Leighann Dobbs:

Blackmoore Sisters
Cozy Mystery Series
* * *

Dead Wrong
Dead & Buried
Dead Tide

— — — — — — —

Lexy Baker
Cozy Mystery Series
* * *

Killer Cupcakes
Dying For Danish
Murder, Money and Marzipan
3 Bodies and a Biscotti
Brownies, Bodies & Bad Guys
Bake, Battle & Roll
Wedded Blintz

— — — — — — —

Dobbs "Fancytales"
Regency Romance Fairytales Series
* * *

Something In Red
Snow White and the Seven Rogues
Dancing On Glass
The Beast of Edenmaine

— — — — — — —

Contemporary Romance

* * *

Sweet Escapes
Reluctant Romance

A Note From The Author

I hope you enjoyed reading this book as much as I enjoyed writing it. This is the fourth book in the Blackmoore sisters mystery series and I have a whole bunch more planned!

The setting for this book is a fictional old west Ghost town. Dead Water doesn't exist in real life (only my imagination). I created it after doing research on various 'real-life' ghost towns, so if some of it sounds familiar, that might be why.

The first three books in the series are based on one of my favorite places in the world - Ogunquit Maine. Of course, I changed some of the geography around to suit my story, and changed the name of the town to Noquitt but the basics are there. Anyone familiar with Ogunquit will recognize some of the landmarks I have in the book.

Also, if you like cozy mysteries, you might like my book *"Brownies, Bodies & Bad Guys"* which is part of my Lexy Baker cozy mystery series. I have an excerpt from it at the end of this book.

This book has been through many edits with several people and even some software programs, but since nothing is infallible (even the software programs) you might catch a spelling error or mistake and, if you do, I sure would appreciate it if you let me know - you can contact me at *lee@leighanndobbs.com.*

Oh, and I love to connect with my readers so please do visit me on facebook at *http:// www.facebook.com/leighanndobbsbooks* or at my website *http://www.leighanndobbs.com.*

Are you signed up to get notifications of my latest releases and special contests? Go to: *http:// www.leighanndobbs.com/newsletter* and enter your email address to signup - I promise never to share it and I only send emails every couple of weeks so I won't fill up your inbox.

***

Excerpt From Brownies, Bodies and Bad Guys:

Lexy sat at one of the cafe tables next to the picture window in her bakery, *The Cup and Cake,* admiring how the princess cut center stone of her engagement ring sparkled in the midmorning sunlight. She sighed with contentment, holding her hand up and turning the ring this way and that as she marveled at the rainbow of colors that emerged when it caught the light at different angles.

Her thoughts drifted to her fiance, Jack Perillo. Tall, hunky and handsome, her heart still skipped a beat when he walked in the room even though they'd been dating for over a year. Lexy had met Jack, a police detective in their small town, when she'd been accused of poisoning her ex-boyfriend. She'd been proven innocent, of course, and she and Jack had been seeing each other ever since. And now they were getting married.

Movement on the other side of the street caught her attention, pulling her away from her thoughts. Her eyes widened in surprise—it was Jack! *What was he doing here?*

Lexy felt a zing in her stomach. Jack wasn't alone. Lexy's eyes narrowed as she craned her neck to get a better look. He was with a woman. A tall, leggy blonde who was clinging to him like tissue paper clings to panty hose.

Lexy stood up pressing closer to the window, her joy in the ring all but forgotten. Her heart constricted when she saw how the leggy blonde was pawing at Jack, giggling up into his face. *Who the hell was she?* They looked very familiar with each other. Clearly Jack knew her ... and it seemed he knew her well.

Jack and the blonde started to walk down the street, out of view. Lexy pushed herself away from the window, stumbling over a chair in her haste to get to the doorway. She spun around, righting the chair, then turned, sprinting toward the door.

She reached out for the handle, jerking back in surprise as the door came racing toward her, almost smacking her in the face.

Standing in the doorway was her grandmother, Mona Baker, or Nans as Lexy called her. But instead of her usual cheery appearance, Nans looked distraught. Lexy could see lines of anxiety creasing her face and her normally sparkly green eyes were dark with worry.

Lexy's stomach sank. "Nans, what's the matter?"

"Lexy, come quick," Nans said, putting her hand on Lexy's elbow and dragging her out the door. "Ruth's been arrested!"

***

"Arrested? For what?" Lexy asked, as Nans propelled her down the street toward her car.

"Nunzio Bartolli was found dead. They think Ruth might have something to do with it!"

Lexy wrinkled her brow. Ruth was one of Nans's best friends. They both lived at the retirement center in town and along with two of their other friends, Ida and Helen, they amused themselves by playing amateur detective solving various crimes and mysteries. The older women were full of spunk and could be a handful, but Lexy had a hard time believing any of them would be involved in a murder. They thrived on *solving* murders, not *committing* them.

"What? How would Ruth even know him?" Lexy opened the door to her VW beetle and slipped into the driver's seat as Nans buckled up in the passenger seat.

"Nunzio was a resident at the Brook Ridge Retirement Center."

Lexy raised her brows. "He was? I heard he had ties to organized crime."

"Well, I don't know about that. He seemed like a nice man." Nans shrugged, then waved her hand. "Now let's get a move on!"

Lexy pulled out into the street, glancing over at the area where she had seen Jack. She slowed down as she drove by, craning her neck to look down the side street where she thought they had gone, but they were nowhere to be seen.

"Can you speed it up? Ruth needs us." Nans fidgeted in the passenger seat.

"Right. Sorry." Lexy felt a pang of guilt. Of course, helping Ruth was more important than finding out what Jack was up to. It was probably nothing but her overactive imagination anyway. Lexy decided to push the leggy blonde from her mind and focus on Ruth.

"So what happened?"

"I'm not really sure. Ida said the police knocked on Ruth's door early this morning and took her in," Nans said, then turned sharply in her seat. "We should call Jack and see if he can help her. Why didn't I think of that before?"

Lexy's stomach clenched at the sound of her fiance's name. She wasn't sure if she wanted to call Jack right now, especially with the image of him and the blonde fresh in her mind. *Should she confront him or let it slide?*

If it was innocent, which it probably was, she'd just make a fool out of herself by confronting him. It was probably a good idea to let some time pass before she talked to him. Lexy was afraid her impulsive nature might cause her to blurt something out she might regret later.

"Hopefully, he'll be at the station. I should call Cassie back at the bakery though, and tell her I've gone out for a while. She'll probably be wondering where I disappeared to." Lexy picked up her cell phone just as she pulled into the parking lot at the police station.

Nans jumped out of the car before she even had it in park. "I'll see you in there."

Lexy watched in amusement as the sprightly older woman sprinted into the station, her giant purse dangling from her arm. She felt sorry for any officer that might try to prevent her grandmother from seeing Ruth.

She made a quick call to Cassie, letting her know where she was and that she'd fill her in later. Then she made her way into the lobby behind Nans.

Nans was talking to Jack's partner, police detective John Darling, who nodded at Lexy as she joined them.

"Ruth isn't arrested!" Nans smiled at Lexy.

Lexy raised an eyebrow at John.

"We just had her in for questioning," John explained.

"Why?"

John rubbed his chin with his hand. "We found her fingerprints and some of her personal effects in Nunzio Bartolli's condo."

Nans gasped. "What? How would those get in there?"

John winked, pushing himself away from the wall he was leaning against. "You'll have to ask Ruth that."

Lexy stared after him as he walked over to the reception desk, his long curly hair hung in a ponytail down his back which swung to the side as he leaned his tall frame over the counter to look at something on the computer. "Actually, she's free to go now. I'll bring her out here if you guys want."

"Please do," Nans said, then turned to Lexy. "Isn't that wonderful? I was so worried."

Lexy nodded as she watched John disappear through the door that led to the offices inside the station. John and her assistant Cassie had been married this past spring and she'd gotten to know him fairly well. She wondered if she should ask him if he knew anything about the blonde she had seen Jack with but didn't want to seem like she was prying into Jack's business.

Lexy shook her head. She needed to stop thinking about the blonde. She trusted Jack. They were getting married, for crying out loud, and she didn't want to be one of those wives who kept her husband on a short leash. The best thing for her to do was to forget all about it.

The door opened and Ruth came out. Nans rushed over giving her a hug. Lexy felt her shoulders relax, relieved that Ruth wasn't in trouble.

"Oh, thanks for coming," Ruth said to Nans and Lexy.

"No problem," Lexy said. "Shall we go? I can drive you guys back to the retirement center, if you want."

"That would be wonderful," Nans said as the three of them made their way to the door. Lexy held it open for the two older women, then followed them out into the summer sunshine.

Ruth breathed in a deep breath of fresh air. "It's good to be outside. For a while there I was a little worried I might be spending my golden years in a cell."

"Why would you think that? Surely you had nothing to do with Nunzio's murder?" Nans raised her eyebrows at Ruth as they walked to Lexy's car.

"Of course I didn't! But they did have some evidence that pointed to me," Ruth said, as she folded herself into Lexy's back seat.

"That's what John said." Lexy slipped into the driver's seat angling the rear view mirror so she could look at Ruth. "What was that all about?"

Lexy saw Ruth's cheeks turn slightly red.

Nans turned in her seat so she could look at Ruth, too. "John said they found your fingerprints and personal effects in Nunzio's condo. How is that possible?"

Ruth turned an even darker shade of red and looked down at her lap, pretending to adjust her seatbelt. "I was in his condo."

"What?" Nans and Lexy said at the same time.

Ruth looked up. Her eyes met Lexy's in the mirror then slid over to look at Nans. "I was seeing Nunzio. Actually, I went there quite regularly. So, naturally, my fingerprints were all over his condo. I was there last night and I must have left a pair of earrings there that the police were somehow able to trace to me."

Nans gasped. "You were there last night? The night he was murdered?"

Ruth nodded. "Yes, I was. But don't worry. I assure you Nunzio was *very* much alive when I left."

***

Find out where you can buy Brownies, Bodies & Bad Guys at my website:

http://www.leighanndobbs.com